ACROSS
THE
CIMARRON

FIRST EDITION, 2016

Across the Cimarron
© 2016 by Jerry Wilson

ISBN 978-0-9903204-8-7

Cover Art
The Opening of Oklahoma 1889 "The Land Run"
Photographer Unknown.
Oklahoma Historical Society Collection, Courtesy of the
Oklahoma Historical Society: #22387.1

Author Photo
@Norma Wilson, 2015.
Taken in the Black Elk Wilderness of the Black Hills.

This publisher is a proud member of

[clmp]

COUNCIL OF LITERARY MAGAZINES & PRESSES
w w w . c l m p . o r g

ACROSS THE CIMARRON

Jerry Wilson

MONGREL EMPIRE PRESS
NORMAN, OKLAHOMA, UNITED STATES OF AMERICA

2016

ACKNOWLEDGMENTS

This is a story of western Oklahoma, and particularly of the people west of the Cimarron River. The story begins with the remnants of the Cheyenne and Arapaho nations who survived abuse and hunger in Colorado and the 1864 Sand Creek Massacre led by Colonel John Chivington. The 1867 Treaty of Medicine Lodge moved them to Oklahoma Territory, to land that extended from the Cimarron to the Texas line. Two decades later the Dawes Act, or the General Allotment Act, required them to choose 160 acres per family so that the rest—most of their land— could be given to settlers.

On April 19, 1892, in the second great Land Run into Oklahoma Territory, settlers poured into Cheyenne-Arapaho land by the thousands, landless Yankees and Southerners and a few former slaves and descendants of slaves. When the dust settled, most every man or head of household over the age of twenty-one had claimed 160 acres of land, almost for free. But in ways not measurable in dollars and cents, the settlers would earn the land in struggle and sweat and often tears. Two of my great grandfathers made the run. One pair of grandparents lived the 65 years covered by this story, until they died in the great Cimarron flood of 1957. As a boy I heard their stories. And in their own old age, two daughters of pioneers, my grandmothers, wrote memoirs that filled many gaps.

I grew up near the Cimarron, roamed its wildness, swam in languid summer pools, watched as the great flood bore away all manner of things made by man on a raging mile-wide torrent. For more than half a century I lived with images seen and heard, meanwhile learning details of history from more objective sources. Over decades the story in your hands began to emerge. It is a story that to the best of my knowledge is accurate and true to details of Oklahoma Territory, and after 1907, statehood. The characters and most of the plot are fictional, though influenced by my ancestors' experience and tales. Without both strains the story could not have been told. Chapter Two is a variation on my story "A Change of Worlds," borrowed from my book of Oklahoma stories, *Blackjacks and Blue Devils*, published by Mongrel Empire Press in 2011.

    I dedicate this book to the peoples whose lives inspired it—to my own pioneering ancestors, to their African American neighbors and most of all to the Cheyenne and Arapaho peoples and their descendants whose lives and cultures still enrich the land on which they once were sovereign. I further dedicate it to my wife, Norma, who when we were much younger "homesteaded" with me on a remote scrap of the Great Plains, and who, along with my brother Paul, cheerfully reads everything I write and makes helpful suggestions. And, of course, to modern pioneers of another sort, those who seek to live in harmony with the natural world and with human neighbors around the world.

ACROSS THE CIMARRON

CHAPTER 1

The boom jerked Reuben Westerfield to consciousness and the blinding flash seared his eyes through the lids. His ringing ears registered the snap of a splitting tree trunk, a long ripping swoosh, a crashing thud.

His now wide eyes began to focus. His hair felt on fire and his skin tingled with electricity. He threw off the quilt and strained to pull himself out of bed. Then came a new sound—water dripping, then running, what sounded like a waterfall above his head. It had rained for two days, and all night it had poured, but this was more than steady drumming on the roof and splashing from the eaves. Now water streamed from the ceiling onto the bed, drenching his legs. Another bolt lighted the sky, outlining a jagged hole in the roof. A huge trunk sprawled across the rafters. Above the bed hung a newly-leafed cottonwood branch.

Ruth was struggling out of bed too, groping for the lamp switch. The power was dead. Reuben swung his legs to the floor and groped in darkness for the overalls he'd draped across the chair. He worked his legs in, pulled on his brogans without socks and felt his way to Ruth's side of the bed.

Now his nose caught the scent—and his eyes the flicker—of burning wood. The lightning strike had done more than bring the cottonwood down. Water that poured through the ceiling reflected a throbbing yellow haze. Despite the driving rain, the attic was on fire! "We've got to get out!" he shouted. He found Ruth's arm and helped her pull on her dress and get her shoes.

They stumbled to the kitchen. It was dry. Reuben flipped another switch, but there was no light. He fumbled in a kitchen drawer and found the flashlight. The batteries were nearly dead. He scooped up a handful of wooden matches and dropped them in the bib of his overalls. On the back porch they pulled on raincoats and overshoes. Reuben gripped Ruth's arm and they plunged into the deluge.

Wind drove rain into their faces. The yard glowed with the pulsing light of the burning roof. Glancing back Reuben saw that the cottonwood, already mature when he'd built the house in its shade so long ago, had split down the middle. The west trunk still dipped and swayed with the storm, the other half draped across the house. Wind-whipped flames fed hungrily on the still-dry rafters.

The pair sloshed through puddles and mud in the slanting rain, then edged down a slippery slope and entered the barn through the open hay door. It was the middle of May, not yet haying season, but they'd sold all the cows except Rosie years ago, so there was still a stack of bales. Guided by lightning strikes they made their way to the pile and collapsed on the hay. Huddled together they watched the battle they had escaped. Would water quench the flames, or would the inferno take their home? Reuben drew his trembling wife close. Neither spoke.

Suddenly Ruth bolted straight. "I'm going back," she declared, straining to escape his grip. "I can't let the pictures and the Bible burn!"

"I'm afraid it's too late," Reuben said, holding her tight. "It wouldn't be safe to go back in. But maybe the rain will put out the fire before they burn."

"Let me go!" she shouted. "We've got to get them out." Reuben was surprised by her strength, how hard she was to hold.

"It's too late!" he repeated. "The fire is already eating toward the kitchen. The whole house is full of smoke."

"I don't care," Ruth insisted. "I'm not going to let them burn!"

"All right, I'll go then!" Reuben barked. "You wait here." He released his hold and plunged back into the driving rain. Ascending the muddy slope was more difficult than going down. He slipped and almost fell, then edged sideways up to level ground and made his way to the crackling ruin. Smoke poured from the kitchen door when he opened it, but he held his breath and groped his way to the buffet where the family album and Bible were kept. He grabbed them and was almost out the door and out of breath when another bolt lighted the room and he saw his fiddle hanging by the door. He gripped the books in his left hand, grabbed the fiddle with his right and burst out of the burning house, leaving the door whipping in the wind.

Finally he reached the hay stack and dropped beside Ruth, gasping for air. "Here are the things you wanted," he said when breath returned. "The house is done, I'm afraid, but at least we're safe, and we can rebuild. We've done that more than once, you know." Then he thought of the phone. Probably the line was down, or if not, then shorted out by rain, but he wished they'd tried it before they fled the house. Maybe he could have reached a neighbor, or maybe even John. Too late now. He realized they hadn't heard from John and Prairie Star for maybe a week. He was glad their home was safe, built well above the river on the bluff Reuben had claimed.

Rain roared on the sheet iron roof of the barn. Wind whipped the trees and jerked at a loose corner of tin. Ruth and Reuben huddled and watched the flames devour their home. "It was a good house," Ruth said at last, "the best we ever had."

"Yes," Reuben replied. "We built it strong. I thought it would outlast us, but I never considered fire. Yes, it was a fine house." It was half a century old, but the first in the neighborhood with modern conveniences, water piped in from the well, even a bathroom, and now it was ruined beyond repair. "But we will rebuild," he said again when he had gathered the strength. "That was our fourth house, you know, if you consider the dugout a house." Then he was sorry he'd mentioned the early abodes, for no doubt the allusion to their first shelters would trigger in Ruth as it always did the sadness that almost buried them there.

The confidence Reuben expressed about rebuilding was far greater than he felt. This fourth house he had built in his prime, and the first three were simple tasks, the dugout a mere gouging of a shallow gully at the edge of the bluff, covered with willow branches and a canvas tarp. The soddy was warm and sound, except for the roof. If only they'd had money for a tight roof, who knows, things might have turned out differently. The log house, too, was easy for a young man with the strength to cut and haul trees from the Gloss Mountains, a man who could raise a whole log above his head and set it in place.

The house that now was crashing, rafter by rafter to the earth, he'd built the year Oklahoma became a state. They'd finally saved enough money from farming and blacksmithing and building other people's houses, and even a dollar here and there from teaching music lessons, that he could build a proper house for Ruth and John. This house he'd built, not on the bluff, but snuggled in the valley near the river where the grove of cottonwoods had shaded summer evenings and protected them from the wind that never seemed to cease.

"I can't believe it's come to this," Ruth muttered. "After all those years when rain wouldn't come, now everything is destroyed by lightning and rain."

Reuben did not reply. It wasn't the first time a dry spell that stretched for years was suddenly quenched by a violent storm. But Ruth was right. Funny how once the drought was broken, the rain wouldn't stop. Yet in their sixty-five years by the river, he'd never seen such a rain as this. March and April had been wetter than normal, and it seemed that this year might be the end of dry weather. Rains had come even more frequently in May, but nothing like this. What was today? It must be the early hours of morning, so that would make it the 16th. He'd emptied the gauge twice yesterday, four inches the first time and five inches and running over before bed, and it had poured all night. He'd heard on the radio that heavy rain was widespread across the Cimarron watershed—western Oklahoma, Kansas and New Mexico.

Now it seemed there was more smoke than flame. "Well, it looks like the rain may be putting out the fire," Reuben said at last. Ruth did not answer, but she surely knew as well as he that the house was ruined. Most of the north roof was gone, and fire smoldered and ate lazily at whatever was still dry in the kitchen end. They waited in silence, the wind and the pounding overhead accented by occasional bumping sounds in the milk cow's stall. Somewhere in the hay a bewildered cat mewed.

Gradually Reuben became aware that Rosie had begun to low in a manner that suggested distress. He heard the moans vaguely for several minutes, preoccupied as he was by sadness and fatigue, and by the growing awareness that nearing the end of his ninth decade of life he would be compelled to start over once more. But gradually Rosie's whimper elevated to a bawl that he could no longer ignore. He pulled himself up from the bale and groped through darkness across a layer of bales toward Rosie's stall.

When he stepped off the last bale, his feet sloshed into water. He stopped in his tracks. This could mean only one thing: the river was not only out of its banks, but was filling the barn! The barn door faced west toward the house, the back toward the river, so he could not have known that in the darkness of night the river had risen far higher than ever before.

Reuben plunged through shin deep water to Rosie's stall. The usually docile cow was agitated, not knowing how to respond to a phenomenon she had never encountered. Reuben reached and found her nose and stroked it until she became calm. Reuben felt anything but calm. This was not the first time he'd seen the Cimarron flood—in fact, there had been many a threatening spring rise—but nothing like this. The worst was the time the railroad bridge washed out and the train plunged into the flood. When the waters receded several days later, Reuben had stabbed an eighty-pound catfish with a pitchfork, dragged it from the slough where it was stranded, carried it up the bluff over his shoulder, cut it up and made the rounds of the neighbors with big hunks of meat. There were other floods too, but never had the waters risen to engulf, or even threaten the barn. Reuben opened the back door of the barn, then the gate of Rosie's stall. The cow bellowed once and plunged into darkness and rain.

Reuben wondered what time it was. Too bad he'd taken his pocket watch out of his overalls when they went to bed. But despite the torrent and the heavy sky, he thought he could see vaguely in the east the first hint of morning. He had no idea what time the lightning had struck, nor how long they'd huddled in the barn, but if that was the glow of dawn, it must be approaching six o'clock. It was hard to be sure in such dim light, but it seemed that the usually lazy Cimarron now stretched as far as he could see, a massive lake that extended more than a mile across the plain to the blackjack dunes. Shaken by this discovery, Reuben picked his way back to the bale where Ruth sat quietly weeping, transfixed by the smoldering remains of home.

Even in the dim light Reuben could see the trouble in her eyes. She'd seen plenty of trouble, and for some of it he'd never stopped blaming himself. But now, except for muted sobs she was quiet, not fretting as she normally would have about what she could provide for breakfast or where they might sleep that night. The silence troubled him more than the turbulence he'd sometimes known. Now her eyes seemed oddly clouded, vacant, staring as if at the empty space that stood between them and the smoking ruin. But Ruth's eyes weren't what they used to be, and he realized now that she'd left her glasses behind. Apparently she was not yet aware of what he had seen. Reuben decided that once daylight came he'd walk up the road to the Webers for help.

Gradually the light grew less dim. Reuben picked out a rose bush beside the driveway and trained his eye on the silhouette. Ten minutes passed, and it was clear that the water continued to rise. The lake between them and the house was widening, and now he could follow its slow creep up the incline. Their small stack of bales had become an island in a growing sea. The water was not yet deep enough that they could not escape, but the deluge continued, and who knew how much water the river's tributaries might be feeding in. How much deeper could it get? He gathered the things he'd brought from the house and set them on a higher bale.

Suddenly Ruth's dim eyes grasped what Reuben had been watching. She jerked rigid with a little cry. "Reuben, the river is flooding!" she croaked. "We have to get out of here."

"Don't worry Ruth," he said, clutching her shoulders in his hands. We have lots of hay. We can stack it higher and stay above the flood." But he wasn't so sure. He envisioned the plain that stretched from where they sat on the bales to the far side of the river, the string of sand dunes that rose much higher than the plain, a bank that would stop further spread to the east. If the river continued to rise it could only come this way. How much longer could it rain? How much had fallen in the Panhandle and the upriver states? Given the force of rain overnight, another five inches must have come on top of the nine he'd dumped. That would be well over a foot of water, and it continued to pour. Reuben glanced toward the lilac bushes north of the house. He couldn't make out the stone that marked the grave Ruth had insisted they move when they rebuilt beside the river, but the lilacs were still well above water.

When he thought about their move he always felt a tinge of guilt about the valley land. Yes, he'd paid good money for it in 1904, money saved from the first good crops and from long hours at his blacksmith forge. But sometimes, especially at night when wind whispered through the cottonwoods, he found himself imagining that he heard voices, murmuring in a language he could not understand. Reuben was not superstitious, and he certainly didn't believe in ghosts. He had never shared his secret shame with anyone, but neither had he quite escaped the haunting feeling that this land, more certainly than the land he'd gained in the run, was tainted by illegitimacy, or that the process by which he acquired it had left a stain that could not be washed away. Perhaps it was the presence of Prairie Star that would not allow him to forget that it was the land her grandfather had chosen, land he lost through sleight of hand.

Now it was clear that building by the riverside might have been unwise for other reasons. When they built in 1907 he had chosen a site several feet above the flood waters of 1905, and everybody assumed that was as bad as it would ever get. Obviously not.

Perhaps it would be prudent to get out of the barn, he thought. But where would they go? There was no other shelter from the still pouring rain. Not the house, that was certain. The chicken house, the tool shed and the smoke house were all even lower than the barn. There was enough light now to see that only the long unused outhouse stood above water, but that would be a cramped, unpleasant refuge.

Water was creeping up the second bale, nearly two feet deep in the barn. He'd built the barn on a rise a couple of feet higher than the surroundings, so that meant the water outside was probably chest deep by now. He could restack the bales and gain a couple more feet of elevation, or they could wade through the water to the driveway and walk the mile to the Weber place, where Peter and Esther's grandson and his family now lived.

While he was considering the bleak options before them, the chicken house rose silently off its foundation and began to float across the yard. "We've got to get out of here," Ruth shrieked. "There goes the chicken house. We're going to drown!" She jerked from his arms, grabbed the Bible in one hand and the album in the other and plunged into the water. Reuben tried to catch her, but he was too late. Now she was out the barn door and up to her chest in water, holding the books in extended hands. Her dress floated around her in the churning water, a flowery halo about her head. Reuben snatched his fiddle from the bale and plunged in behind her. He had almost reached her when she slipped, began to thrash against the water, and disappeared below the foam.

Panicked, Reuben strode as fast as he could against the current toward her. She resurfaced a few feet in front of him, choking and gasping for air. Her flailing hands were empty. Reuben flung the fiddle away and dived toward her. He came up grasping the hem of her dress. He pulled her to him and clutched her to his breast. His foot touched earth, but they were on the slope, and water was almost over his head. His foot slipped, and they both went down.

"Swim for the chicken house!" he shouted. Reuben thrashed at the muddy water, and Ruth too began to stroke, and little by little they closed the gap between them and the bobbing roof. After what seemed an eternity Reuben reached and grabbed the slippery edge and held on. He pulled Ruth to him, and together they floated with their life buoy until their panting subsided.

"We have to get on the roof," Ruth gasped. Reuben pulled with all his might and finally raised himself high enough to topple over onto the slippery shingles. Digging his fingers into the soft cedar he pulled himself up, then tugged until Ruth's knee caught the edge, and he dragged her up. They sprawled on the roof, inched toward the peak and lay gasping for breath in the driving rain.

"Now we've lost everything we'd saved," Ruth lamented, and she began to sob. "The Bible, the pictures, even the fiddle. We might as well have gone down with them. The whole past is lost. Even the music is gone."

Finally Reuben raised onto his elbows to survey their circumstances. The barn and house were disappearing in smoke and rain. He scanned the dark muddy waters, wondering if the books might float. He assumed they would not, and even if they spotted the lost treasures, there would be no safe way to get them back.

"There's my fiddle!" he exclaimed.

"Where?" Ruth asked.

"Look, just over there," he said, pointing to a scrap of debris floating in the foam. "At least I think it is. If only I had something to reach it with." He raised higher and squinted across the dark water. Was it the fiddle, or some other floating scrap of wood? He couldn't be sure, so he kept his eye trained on the object. Little by little the current took it away.

"Well, it doesn't really matter," he said at last. "I guess the Bible and the pictures are lost for sure, but I can make a new fiddle. Right after we build a new house." He forced a little chuckle.

They were soaked to the bone, but at least their raincoats provided some protection against the wind. They clutched each other, and finally their chattering teeth were still. Light grew stronger, and now Reuben could distinguish the reddish brown water of the river from the gray of the sky. He scanned the horizon for landmarks, but everything seemed strange. Never in sixty-five years had he seen the river country from this point of view. Only the broad strokes were obvious, the bluff above which lay their homestead and first homes, and far to the east the sand hills that no doubt in some distant past blew up from the river bed. But for the first time, at least since 1892, the dunes had become the river's bank.

Even when he made the first run in 1889 Reuben had heard that the Cimarron could be treacherous. He'd read somewhere that the river was named by the Spanish explorer Coronado, who crossed it in 1541 on his journey to a place called Quivira in what became Kansas. Cimarron was a Spanish word that meant wild or unruly, people said. Some said the word referred to a wild animal, perhaps wild sheep, or maybe an escaped slave.

Reuben had certainly found that the name fit the river. The flood of 1905 stood out, of course, when the railroad bridge washed out and the freight train plunged into the swirling water. The engineer rode a bridge plank to the island below Reuben's claim, caught his foot on barbed wire and hung on, shouting himself hoarse before John finally heard him. Reuben and John had built a crude boat and rowed out to rescue the man.

For sixty-five years he and Ruth had swum in the river. When John was a boy, and later Joseph, they caught perch and catfish, watered their cows, and more than once walked across a bed of blowing sand. But nothing in his experience had prepared him for today.

Reuben glanced back up the river behind them. Their home and its sheltering grove had disappeared in the rain, and now even the familiar bluff was vague in the distance. They clung precariously to the small bobbing structure, their lifeboat, still shivering in the early morning chill. Clinging to the roof ridge with one hand and to Ruth with the other, Reuben closed his eyes. He remembered the first time he'd crossed the Cimarron.

CHAPTER 2

Reuben pushed aside his blanket and raised to an elbow, his body stiff from sleeping on cold ground, and from the fifteen miles he'd walked that day from Hennessey. He opened his canteen and drank. Fires flickered or blazed as far as he could see down the Cimarron. Figures crouched or moved amongst the shadows, silhouetted against the smoky orange glow. Reuben stretched his back and got to his knees. Peering at the still shapes in the starlight around him, he strapped the canteen to his belt, then rolled his food box, tools, blanket, potatoes and the Colt revolver into his tarp. He tucked in the ends and cinched the bundle with a scrap of rope.

In the makeshift tent behind him a baby cried. Reuben stood and picked up his roll. The blanket door of the lean-to flapped aside and a man came out. "Baby got a fever," the man said. "You folks hasn't got medicine does you?"

"Sorry," Reuben said. "It's just me and I'm traveling light."

"Thankee sir," the man said. He picked up a stick and stirred the coals of a smoldering fire, reddening his patched overalls and charcoal face. "She been sick since Fort Smith, but now she worse," he said. He shook his head and raised his eyes to the west. "I sho do hope to get a piece of that lan. Maybe she be aright when we there."

"Yeah," Reuben said. "Don't we all. I hope she'll be O.K."

"Hey knock off the chatter, darkie," snarled a voice from a clump of willows to Reuben's south. "I can't believe they're lettin you niggers run anyhow. There's more hard-workin white men than there is land, folks that can make somethin out of this."

"The good book say the meek shall inherit the earth," the black man answered. He crawled back into his tent. The baby was quiet now.

The other man crouched in the bushes and touched an ember to a cigarette, illuminating a lean and whiskered face. "Damn Indians don't need this land," he said. "These Cheyennes and Arapahos ain't even from here I heard. This is just where they stuck em. Reservation, they call it. Well I got reservations myself." His laugh turned to a hacking cough and he spat.

"Been over have you?" Reuben said in a low voice. He squinted for a better look at the man.

"Hell yes, ain't you?" The man sounded surprised. "They got more than they can use anyhow, the claim agent said so. Surplus land. What the hell, Indians don't know the value of land. What this territory needs is white farmers and cattlemen. Why let four million acres of good farm land go to waste?"

"Makes sense," Reuben said. He turned his back and waited for the other man to disappear. A sudden gust whipped a flurry of sparks from the negro's fire.

When Reuben glanced back the other man was not in sight. His ankle still smarting from his leap from the train, he crept through the willows to the water's edge. He found a hole under a tangle of roots and shoved his bundle in. He ventured into the river, his eye on the western bluff. He waded until the water reached his armpits. Campfires and starlight reflected from the smooth surface. He edged against the current until water touched his neck.

The Cimarron bed was wide and no doubt usually shallow, but in April it was high. The water was cold, and he began to swim, half floating, the gentle flow carrying him along. Finding the bottom, he waded toward shore. He came out dripping on a sandbar and plunged quickly into another dome of willows.

He crouched shivering in a little clearing, the bluff looming high in the western sky. "Upland might be dry," he muttered to himself, "but it's bound to grow wheat." He was glad he had seed back in Kansas.

Reuben picked out the north star. He stumbled onto a trail of sorts, and followed it south. Deer? No, the brush was cleared too high. Had to be Indians. He'd heard some were still around. Unhappy with their allotments, apparently. But they got first choice, the papers said, and they were paid for the rest. He hoped it was true.

Reuben recalled the other run in '89, to the "unassigned lands." God, what a place that was. He'd staked a good claim, maybe fifty miles downstream from here. He'd had Charley then, and Charley was fast, Texas racehorse stock. He chuckled, picturing the others eating Charley's dust. He'd slept that night under these same stars, his future secure. He couldn't wait to bring Ruth to those gentle hills, the bottom land, the spring, the big native grass. But at sunrise he woke in the shadow of a dirty ragged man, a double-barreled shotgun poked in his face. He could still smell the cold oily steel. It had been a long ride back to Kansas. He'd gambled everything, but lost his claim. He should have brought a gun.

The trail veered away from the river and ran closer to the bluff. It was dark in the brush, and a branch lashed his face. He raised his arm as a shield and plunged on. It was a matter of hours now, after three long years. Ruth would be happy again if they could just settle down. Maybe have some kids. She'd never complained, and she didn't blame him. But she was tired of moving, always packing or unpacking the trunk, him blacksmithing in Hutchinson, laying rails in Wichita, bucking bundles clear to Fort Dodge, carpentering when he got the chance, but always moving and waiting, like thousands of others, waiting for another run.

All summer he'd harvested wheat, a record crop, but for other men. But bust his gut as he had, they'd saved just thirty dollars. He'd need twelve up front to file on a claim, so that didn't leave a lot. At least he'd gleaned some seed wheat, enough for twenty acres. But then he'd lost Charley, which narrowed his options. Funny how a step in a gopher hole could change a man's fate. He was on foot this time, but he did have the Colt.

The path petered out in towering cottonwoods and hackberries, but Reuben kept his southerly course. Then suddenly the flat broke off and he plunged down a bank to a stream. He knelt and dipped his hand to drink. The water tasted salty.

Instead of crossing the creek he turned up the north bank and followed it west. The bed rose steadily into a canyon of blackjacks and then ash, and in ten minutes he emerged from the trees into open prairie, a world of stars and grass. Reuben strode back north across the plain, his legs swishing through lush buffalo grass and bluestem. He mounted a ridge, then descended to another stream, much smaller, likely a tributary of the salty creek. He tasted again, and the water was cold and sweet. The spring had to be near. He followed this stream past wild plums, their hominy-smelling blossoms glowing white against the dark plain. A shallow valley sloped toward him.

Reuben found the spring in a jumble of rocks amidst a grove of trees and dropped to his knees. "Spring Creek," he said out loud, and he rolled back his head and laughed to the stars. "It might not be original, but Spring Creek it is." He thrust his hands into the damp soil and squeezed a ball of sticky mud between his fingers. "God, rich," he said. "Ruth, my dear, this is the place." He washed his hands and face, cupped his hands and took a long drink from the spring. He emptied his canteen and refilled it. He stood and strode back toward the bluff, his steps solid on the mellow soil, the sod he would break to grow wheat.

The prairie sloped gently back toward the bluff, and soon the now dim string of fires came back into view, less than half a mile away. Coming to the edge, he held to a sumac branch and peered over. "Too steep for a wagon," he said with satisfaction, "or even a horse." To get here by horse the route he had come would take time, probably ten or fifteen minutes. But a man on foot could cross the river where it was deep and come straight up this bluff, and faster. He smiled. He would be here first.

Now to find the marker. He followed the bluff north until he found the post, notched to indicate the southeast corner of a quarter section. It was surrounded by a small pile of stones. He crouched by the pile and fingered the stones. They were cold and hard. There weren't enough here for a chimney, but maybe a hearth. Reuben shivered in his still damp clothes. He stood and hurried back the way he had come.

April 19, 1892. Eleven o'clock.

As far as Reuben could see, north or south, there were people, thirty thousand, somebody said. A permanent cloud of dust hung in the humid spring air. Some had been here for days, and they guarded their positions at the water's edge. Between him and the river two men with horses trimmed a hoof with a knife. In the willows beside him the lean man was oiling a big revolver. A nasty scar blazed across the man's cheek, red beneath the dust. The black family to his rear were rolling up their makeshift tent.

Reuben knew that others besides himself and the scarred man had crossed the river and picked a place. Maybe somebody else had picked his. He couldn't get out of his mind that he'd seen fresh hoof tracks by the spring. All he had to do now was get there first. There weren't many like him, on foot. All along the line horses stamped impatiently in the dust or strained against the lines of buckboards, buggies and wagons. Just to his north was a rickety wagon with a woman and five kids, not even a man.

Scar face came out of the willows and stooped to unhobble his big dark roan. He turned the horse toward the river and glanced contemptuously at Reuben. "Where's your horse?" he sneered. "Gonna do her on foot?"

"That's right," Reuben answered. He stared straight into the scornful eyes, wild outlaw eyes it seemed to him, eyes that reminded him of the claim jumper. There were plenty of others like him too. Gamblers and bootleggers had apparently worked the crowd for days, and their pockets were full.

The black man and his boy finished with their scraps of canvas. The woman was washing a cooking pot, the baby fretting listlessly at her breast. Another child drew in the dust with a stick. The family stood out like the black eye of a daisy in a sea of dusty white. "How's the baby?" Reuben asked.

"She not cryin'," the woman replied, "but maybe she cain't no more. We got to get her to a place."

"Just be sure it's nowhere near mine," growled scar face. He advanced as he talked, and Reuben saw that he dragged a foot, like a coyote escaped from a trap. "You darkie sharecroppers think you can run a farm? I doubt it. I'll give you a year and then I'll buy you out. All you dirt scratchers think you're gonna be rich, don't you? Maybe you can grow cotton, but you don't know the first thing about hangin on. Now me, I'm too smart to even try. Pure speculation, that's my line. If the price is high I sell, an if it's low I buy. And free Indian land is about as low as it gets." He laughed and bit off a plug of tobacco.

Reuben turned his back and glanced down the west-facing line. How many here would do anything for a quarter section of land? And it wasn't just the crooks and claim jumpers either. It was men like himself, men who knew the Indian land was nearly gone, that it was now or never. Reuben was glad he'd left Ruth in Kansas. She'd be here soon enough.

It was almost noon. The human snake writhed and strained against the river's edge. The dust cloud hung low over the line, drifting aimlessly north toward Kansas, the place from which lots of others besides Reuben had come, at least most recently. The two men in front tightened their saddle straps. The woman on his right scolded the kids in the wagon to keep them still while she bound a splint to a cracked wagon spoke.

"Need help with that?" Reuben called.

"I'll manage," she said. "Been doing for myself for quite some time now. Thanks anyway." Her face burned red from sun and exertion.

Nervous shouts rang along the river's edge. There was an energy here that Reuben knew, this lust for land. And he knew the poverty, the secret shame, the failures and regrets. But there was fierceness too, the offspring of powerlessness. At noon it would all explode. He'd seen it before, in eighty-nine, the violence, the energy, the thrust. By nightfall it would all be over. Tomorrow this community would still exist, but transformed, something new under the sun. Tent towns up and down the river, wagons crouched and rude shelters built throughout the valleys and the hills. It would no longer be surplus land.

Reuben's watch read five minutes to twelve. He squinted south into the sun, already hot. His eye traced the tree-lined bluff once more, searched the valleys to the south and measured the cottonwoods at the mouth of the salty creek. The bottom land looked good, but it was too far away. As always his eye came to rest where the red cliff rose, almost perpendicular it seemed from here. In less than an hour he would drive his stake. By nightfall his blanket would be stretched over dead branches to form a crude shelter, not to protect him from the night, but so he could fall asleep thinking, "my land."

He would build a dugout, then a sod room, and some day a log or framed house. He wouldn't need a well, at least not now; the spring flowed enough for a garden and trees. Maybe later he'd dig a well and get cattle. On this land they would work and love and have children, and someday, when his children had children, he would lie below the sod.

It was two minutes until noon. The milling and maneuvering was intense, thousands elbowing for position, conversations all but ceased. Horses stamped, and people waited in the heat and dust.

A man in a string tie stood up on a wagon a hundred yards down the river and waved his arms for quiet. He introduced himself as Tom Tayler from Hennessey, the town from which Reuben had walked. He welcomed folks to the territory and explained again the process of staking a claim, which everybody here knew by heart. Somebody handed him a gun.

Reuben checked the rope on his bundle again. He had biscuits and dried meat for a few days, potatoes, water, his papers, his stake, a few tools, and the Colt. The pistol had cost him plenty. Everybody wanted one it seemed. He cinched the bundle tighter and strapped it to his back. He was ready. "Another minute," said a man in front. Reuben gazed straight ahead, concentration centered in his ears and his legs, listening for the shot, ready to run.

The revolver exploded and they were off. Reuben plunged through the willows and into the river, waded until the familiar cold water touched his armpits, then swam, fast this time. His bundle was heavy on his back, but as before, the current tugged him toward his goal. When his feet touched bottom he strained and sloshed to shore and ran, over the sand, through the willows, up the grassy slope to the bluff.

It was even steeper than he thought, and loose. Scrambling uphill with the roll on his back intensified the pain in his ankle, but that he must ignore. He clawed and slipped, tried another spot, and another. Finally he grasped clumps of grass and pulled himself up to the hanging roots of a blackjack oak. Hand over hand he scrambled and pulled until he reached the top. He swung his legs over the edge, stood and sprinted to the pile of stones.

He dropped panting to the earth, stripped off his bundle, untied the rope. He pulled out his stake and stabbed the sharpened point into the red earth. He seized a large stone from the pile to drive it in. His arms were raised to strike when he saw the skull, peering from the pile where he'd taken the stone. The surface was dull, the forehead round, the teeth grinning, one missing in front. From the deep hollow sockets, dark eyes burned into his for an instant and then were gone.

He dropped the boulder. One by one he picked away the stones until the skull was free. He touched its smoothness, then lifted it out. The wide round sockets were empty, unbroken circles, two floating questions over high cheek bones. His own mouth formed another o. "Who?" it asked, and "how?" "What now?" Reuben shook the image from his brain. He knelt by the pile and carefully balanced the skull atop the stones. He picked up the boulder and pounded in his stake.

For the second time in his twenty-four years, Reuben had land. The blue devils that for three years had pursued him would be laid to rest. He sprawled on his back and elbows in the grass, the revolver on his lap. He raised his canteen and took a long drink of Spring Creek water. Eyeing the stones again, he saw that some were charred, perhaps by ancient fires.

Over the southern ridge a dark horse and rider appeared, streaking toward him through a whirlwind of dust, hooves pounding the mellow sod. Reuben remembered the scar-faced man he'd encountered on the other side, and his fingers found the revolver and gripped it tight. As the horse drew near he recognized the roan stallion. The man rode hard, straight toward him, neither slackening nor veering when he saw Reuben by the pile of stones. When he reined hard at last a cloud of dust filled Reuben's eyes. Reuben's finger was on the trigger, the barrel of the revolver aimed at the rider's heart. "So feet are faster than you thought," Reuben said in a voice calm but lethal. "Spur that horse or you're a dead man." The man spat, and without a word, rode on.

When he was gone, Reuben stood to his feet and surveyed the land, the first good look by daylight. "My land," he called out, then louder, "My land!" He glanced back at the pile of blackened stones. His would not be the first fire they had seen. His eyes could not avoid the penetrating gaze of the skull, the searching sockets that mesmerized his brain. "Our land?" he asked. The gentle breeze that wafted up from the river brought no answer but the distant din of horses and wagons and men.

Across the Cimarron

CHAPTER 3

Now they were passing the Bluff that Reuben had scaled so long ago. The sun must be rising, he thought, though it was obscured by clouds and steady rain. In the middle of May mornings should be warm, but their clothing was still wet under their raincoats, and Reuben and Ruth still shivered in the wind-driven rain. He thought he spotted the place he'd ascended, recalled the frantic scramble to the overhanging roots of the blackjack that had long since died and fallen to decay. He wondered if he would see this bluff again.

Yet, with half a mile of navigation behind them, their chance vessel began to seem more secure. The chicken house was small, the roof a gentle single slope, twelve by fourteen feet. Likely the free-standing nests and roosts had floated to just under the roof, which improved buoyancy and stability. The low side of the building was six feet tall, the high side to which they clung, eight. About the bottom half was submerged. But the craft seemed stable, and Reuben told himself that they would survive, that sooner or later the hen house would be driven by the current to one bank or the other, to a place where the water was less than four feet deep, where they would run aground and regain land.

But his sense of the familiar grew ever more vague as they floated beyond the bluff he'd known so well. Reuben had difficulty making out other landmarks, neighbors' fields, fence lines, even clumps of trees. There was, of course, the break where Salt Creek entered, the confluence now buried under water far deeper than a man's head. His eye traced the ravine, saw where he had ascended the slope so long ago, the same hill that Breedlove thundered up. Yes, he'd threatened to kill the would-be claim jumper, and would have done it too, but it was just as likely that

Breedlove would have killed him if he hadn't had the Colt. As usual, Reuben tried to shut the memory out.

Now Reuben realized that besides the low visibility, his view of the bank was dimmed because they were floating ever farther from land, nearer the middle of the raging stream. They were drawn like other scraps of debris to the swirling middle above the channel, a rusty cow tank there, boards and fallen trees, what looked like a bloated cow, buildings and pieces of buildings, anything that would float and that had lifted from its resting place in groves and barnyards for no telling how many miles up stream and converged in the foamy vortex far above the river's usually lazy bed. The river was wider than he had ever seen, in fact wider than any white man had ever seen, well over a mile, he guessed. Even as the light grew stronger, everything on the receding banks grew more dim.

Now they were passing a small clump of willows, their upper branches peeking from the surface and collecting foam and small pieces of floating trash, a bucket, a fence post, scraps of paper. These treetops being the only thing protruding from the reddish waters, Reuben reasoned that they must now be over the island where in the early days he had grazed his cattle, the island where the engineer survived a night in the waters of another frigid spring flood. If only he had the one by four oar he'd used that day, perhaps he could row this unlikely vessel to shore as he had then. But he and Ruth had no paddle, and strangely enough, none of the scraps of debris that floated with them and that might have served that purpose came close enough to grasp. They were at the mercy of the current. They must go where the wild river would take them.

So they watched the island slip by, the island that had been an unexpected bonus to his riverside claim. In spring it often flooded; in fact, a flash flood about 1900 had taken two good young heifers away. But in most years, once the waters receded the island grew a diverse mix of most every kind of seed the waters had borne from above, from sandburs and thistles to alfalfa and various grasses to every spring's new crop of cottonwoods and willows. Summers when water was low the island grew to twenty acres or more, enough to pasture several head of cows or steers.

In the early years, when water was low Reuben or Ruth, and later John drove the cows to the island in the morning and back home to the corral before night. But in 1904 he had fenced the perimeter, which meant the cows could stay there as long as pasture held out. It was the fence that saved the engineer, a man named Palmer if he remembered right.

If there was ever a flood that came close to this one, it was the great flood of 1905. They were in the log house by then. It was small and dark, but snug, with a tight roof and a warm stove, a good place for the Westerfields to weather a violent storm. They had no way of knowing, of course, but about the time they blew out the coal oil lamp that March night, the new railroad bridge a few miles north was about to fail. It had been hastily built, part of a push to extend a new line into western Oklahoma Territory in anticipation of statehood, something all the politicians were talking about. The Indian nations and some of the white residents of the eastern part of what would become Oklahoma— Indian Territory it was called—were lobbying hard to keep the territories divided and make two states, the eastern half named for Sequoyah, who created the Cherokee alphabet. Others, including President Roosevelt, wanted to combine Indian Territory and Oklahoma Territory into a single state with a name that in the Choctaw language meant "red people." The debate ended when Congress approved the single state of Oklahoma in 1907.

But on that spring night in 1905, all of that was irrelevant. Swirling muddy waters were eating hungrily at the pilings on the west edge of the bridge, but no one was there to see. A freight train chugged west in the darkness, dropping from the sage-covered dunes into the wide low valley of the Cimarron. When the headlight's beam reached the bridge, all appeared in order. Even if the engineer could have seen what was happening below the deck, it would have been too late to apply the brakes. The train rolled slowly across the swirling flood until its weight reached the pilings whose footing had been undermined. Without warning the bridge went over and the train plunged into the dark muddy waters of the Cimarron. More than fifty years had passed, but Reuben remembered the man's story as if he'd heard it yesterday.

The locomotive's massive weight bore it immediately to the river's bed. But somehow the engineer and the brakeman—the only passengers on the train—managed to open the door and plunge into the icy water. When they surfaced they were surrounded by debris. They began to swim with the flow, and within moments each man grasped a floating bridge plank. They stayed together as long as they could, but gradually the current swept them apart. Before long neither could hear the other's shouts as down the river they floated.

It wasn't until a couple of days later that anybody heard of the brakeman. He eventually washed into a pile of debris along the bank somewhere near Kingfisher, some twenty miles downstream. But the engineer was luckier. As he floated along in darkness his boot caught on something that stopped his downstream roll. He tugged, and found it firm. After clinging by his foot for some minutes and contemplating his options, Palmer felt along his plank until he found a protruding spike. Grasping the spike with his right hand, he lowered himself below the surface to find what his foot had caught. It was a strand of stiff barbed wire—a fence. The sky was black with rain. There was no way to know where the wire ran, or which way might lead to higher ground.

Clinging to his plank with one hand he inched slowly along the fence, one foot over the other, carefully securing each new footing before releasing the last. Gradually the wire rose nearer the surface, and soon he found a second wire. If this was a typical fence, three barbed wires, he must be within a couple of feet of land. He ventured on, moving east, and in another five minutes his foot touched earth. He waded until at last he found a tiny island of soggy sand. Even then he did not relinquish his plank. If the river continued to rise he might need the life preserver again. But with both feet grounded he felt secure. He heard something rattle. He grabbed a stick and flung a rattlesnake that shared the island into the water. He sat down on his plank to wait for morning. His trusty railroad watch had drowned—it read ten twenty-three—but he had little idea how long it had been stopped. What he did know was that morning was far away, and there was nothing he could do to ease the misery of a night in sodden clothing and driving rain in the middle of a raging river. And yet he felt as if a series of miracles had spared his life. Somehow, for a time he slept.

As day began to dawn the rain slacked, and by sunrise the sky had mostly cleared. He found himself profoundly hungry, and thirsty too. He thought of drinking a handful of the murky water, but decided that should be a last resort. It was a beautiful morning to contemplate the world from a tiny spit of sand in a churning ochre sea. The water had neither risen nor fallen. He saw that he was much closer to the west bank than to the east, and he thought he could see a small house on the horizon, near the water's edge just north of an eroding bluff. Even if it was a house, who knew whether it was inhabited, and anyway it was perhaps half a mile away. To the east he saw nothing but brushy dunes and muddy water. Sitting on his plank he trained his eye on the house.

Not long after the sun rose, a small figure appeared. It seemed to be a woman in a long light dress. He stood and began to shout. The woman stood long and faced the river, then turned and went back into what by daylight appeared to be a small log house. Palmer sat back down on his plank. Before long other figures appeared, a man and a child, a boy he thought. Each time he cried at the top of his lungs, but they didn't seem to hear. They went about their morning chores, the boy bringing in an armload of wood from a little barn, the man disappearing into the barn with a bucket, then reappearing a few minutes later carrying the bucket to the house, from the chimney of which a twist of smoke now rose. He imagined the woman frying bacon and eggs, and his stomach churned.

At last the boy and the man came back out. They went to the barn, and the boy emerged with a cow, a jersey it appeared, on a length of rope. The pair proceeded along the river's swollen edge toward the bluff—toward him! He stood again and began to shout. Then it occurred to him to remove his jacket and he began to wave it wildly above his head.

The boy stopped, and so did the cow. The cow began to graze, but the boy stood perfectly still and gazed toward the river. Was he simply contemplating the flood, or had he noticed the strange phenomenon of a crazy man standing in the middle of the river waving a garment and yelling at the top of his lungs? Then the boy waved back. Palmer had been seen.

The boy tied the rope to a fence post and raced back to the barn. When he reappeared he was with the man. The man began to wave, and the two of them trotted down the incline toward the bluff. The man cupped his hands and shouted across the water. "Hold on. We will come!" And then they retraced their footsteps to the barn.

In a few minutes they reemerged, the man carrying planks on his shoulder, the boy carrying a bucket and tools. At the water's edge they squatted and went to work. For half an hour a hammer pounded. Then they worked in silence. The woman came from the house with a bundle tied in cloth, and finally the man climbed into the crude boat they had constructed, the woman handed him the bundle, and he was off, guiding himself into the current with a one by four.

For a time Palmer thought the man would overshoot the island, but he rowed powerfully, and at last the boat hit sand. Palmer was there to meet him. He pulled the craft higher and the man got out. "Good morning," the rower said. He reached out his hand. "My name is Reuben Westerfield. Here are some things my wife sent for you." He opened the tied cloth and handed the man a jar of milk and a sandwich of bacon in still warm bread.

There were tears in the engineer's eyes. He took the sandwich in one hand, the jar in the other, then grasped Westerfield in his arms and wept. "I didn't think I would see this day," he said. "Thank you for seeing me and coming for me. My name is Paul Palmer. I was the engineer on the train. The bridge washed out. I caught a plank and came here last night." He began to devour the food.

When he had finished, the men launched the boat back onto the flood. It was barely deep enough for two, the sides made of twelve-inch planks, the cracks sealed with tar. The weight of two men lowered the boat to a palm's width above the water. Reuben rowed the blunt craft into the current, but they drifted downstream faster than they closed the gap to land. After a time he handed the one by four to Palmer, who rowed until the boat touched the bank. He leapt out and pulled the boat ashore, and Reuben climbed out. They dragged the vessel onto higher land and walked toward the ribbon of smoke from Ruth's kitchen stove.

Across the Cimarron

CHAPTER 4

The stove was the heaviest thing they'd brought from Kansas, but neither Ruth nor Reuben had regretted for a moment any of the things they'd left behind to fit the stove into the wagon. Safely packed amongst their blankets inside the oven were Reuben's fiddle and their meager family treasures. The fiddle, and also the guitar, were luxuries he sometimes felt almost guilty about having brought, considering what else they did without, but Ruth loved to hear him play, and she scoffed at the idea that the instruments were superfluous. Not that there was that much to leave. They had married in 1890, the year after Reuben's first run, and the stove was their wedding gift from Ruth's parents. It was old even then, but sound, versatile and efficient. It had easily heated the log house, and even in the framed house they would later build, its warmth reached far beyond the kitchen. It was all the heat they needed except on the coldest days.

And yet, comfortable by the stove on a cold winter night in those early days of struggle, Reuben's mind often ranged back to the claim he'd lost in eighty-nine. He sometimes even dreamed about the quarter he had staked on the Cimarron south of where the town of Crescent grew, good river bottom land with tall native grasses, a low promontory back from the river with a grove of native oaks and cottonwoods. That was the place he'd slept the night of April 22, the place he imagined he'd build a home, and where he awakened next morning with a shotgun in his face. But in spite of the setback he and Ruth married anyway, as they had planned, and for the next three years he worked every job he could find, every hour he could give. He worked long days as a carpenter for a house builder on the edge of the growing city of Wichita. Evenings he applied the skills he'd learned from his father back in Tennessee in a part time job at a blacksmith shop. He taught fiddle to a pair of high school students at a dime a lesson. In July he followed the harvest, bucking bundles and threshing wheat. He and Ruth lived in a converted carriage house and grew a garden in the alley. They saved every penny they could, hoping to someday have enough for a down payment on a farm.

In early summer of 1891, a customer at the blacksmith shop told Reuben he'd heard that more Indian land in Oklahoma Territory was to be opened for settlement the next spring. No date had yet been set. The land lay west of the Cimarron River, Cheyenne Arapaho land. With the prospect of essentially free land on the horizon once again, the future looked much brighter. He and Ruth began to plan. He would ride Charley again, of course. Charley was a little older now, but he could still run with the best of them. They saved in hopes of buying a wagon, figuring when the time came they would buy another horse, or perhaps a good plow mule, and once Reuben and Charley had made the run and staked a claim they'd return to Wichita, team Charley with a new mate and haul everything they owned back to the claim. But in July Charley broke his left front leg.

It was Reuben's fault, or at least he blamed himself. He'd ridden Charley to work in wheat fields west of town that week, usually returning after dark. He pushed Charley more than he should have, and in truth, Charley loved to run, especially in the cooler hours of night. Reuben took a short cut across unplowed prairie instead of following the road. Of course he did not anticipate the open gopher hole that Charley hit. The bone snapped just above the ankle. Charley went down, and Reuben hurtled through the darkness for a hard fall.

When he dragged himself up, Charley was whimpering in pain, hobbling on three legs, the fourth bulging at a terrible angle that Reuben knew meant one thing. Charley was done. It was the hardest thing he'd ever had to do, harder even than riding away from the first claim with a shotgun at his back. He walked the limping horse back to the farm where he'd been threshing, borrowed a gun and shot Charley between the eyes. His own eyes streamed tears on the long walk back to Wichita.

So that meant a change of plans. He would have to make the run on foot—if there was another run. For months there had been speculation, but no definite promise, no date set. All winter he worked every hour he could, but found that buying a wagon was out of reach. Instead he searched pawn shops until he found a used Colt revolver, which cost a big chunk of their savings. He and Ruth had few secrets, but this was one. He didn't tell her he'd spent eight dollars for a gun. What happened in eighty-nine wasn't going to happen again.

On April 12 the newspapers announced that the run into Cheyenne-Arapaho land was set for April 19—just a week away! Reuben quit his job and borrowed a wagon and team from Ruth's father. They loaded everything they owned and moved it out of the carriage house and into a back room at Ruth's parents' house.

Now to get to the boundary, the Cimarron. The Chicago, Rock Island and Pacific Railroad had been extended south from Caldwell on the Kansas-Oklahoma Territory line in 1890, following the old Chisholm Trail all the way to the South Canadian River, the border of the Chickasaw Nation. Very early in the morning of April 17, Reuben kissed Ruth goodbye. He strapped his full canteen to his belt and shouldered the things he had packed for the run—a tarpaulin, and rolled inside a blanket, a box of food, a bag of seed potatoes, a few tools and the Colt. By dawn he had walked to the rail yard, where a freight train steamed and rumbled on the tracks. He was not alone. Others who could not afford a ticket were there, waiting for the chance to climb into an empty cattle car that was heading south to pick up another load of beef.

Just after dawn the train began to move. As daylight gradually displaced the shadows, Reuben saw that he shared his car with at least a dozen men, some who looked more desperate than himself, some whose gaze he did not return. He made himself as comfortable as he could on his bundle, his back against the steel.

The train picked up speed, faster than a running horse. Loud talk filled the car, boasts and offers and threats. A gambler took out a deck of cards and stirred up a game. Reuben spoke to no one. His jaw was set, his stare unflinching, offering determination, but for anybody who might challenge him, threat.

The train chugged out of the cow town of Wichita, across acres of tall but still green wheat, through the hill country along the border and into the Cherokee strip.

It was late afternoon when the train left the strip and entered the formerly "Unassigned Lands" that had represented Reuben's hopes three years earlier. Another couple of miles and they rolled into the little town of Hennessey. Every rider clutched his belongings and edged toward the open door.

Reuben had chosen a place at the front of the car, near the door, so he was among the first to jump. He sat on the edge of the floor, watched for a smooth grassy place, tossed out his bundle and dropped to the ground, his feet already in motion to run with the rumbling train. But his legs could not move fast enough to match the momentum of his body. He slid and tumbled down the embankment, coming to a stop a good hundred feet past his bundle. One ankle felt twisted, and when he leapt to his feet pain shot up through the leg. He hobbled fast as he could and grabbed his belongings, then sat in the grass and rubbed his smarting ankle.

As the caboose rolled past, Reuben glanced down the line. Some of the men were up and moving. A few were doubled in pain. He shouldered his bundle and limped away, heading west. At the edge of the bluff just beyond the railroad tracks he crossed a wide strip of hard-packed land, the Chisholm Trail he'd heard so much about, a path denuded and packed hard by hundreds of thousands of cattle driven north from Texas to railheads in Kansas, including the railroad yard he'd left in Wichita.

The initial descent from Hennessey was steep, then the terrain leveled to a gentle slope. He hobbled slowly toward a line of trees that meant a stream of some kind, likely a tributary to the Cimarron. If memory served correctly, a crude map he'd seen called it Turkey Creek. He was pretty sure he couldn't walk far on the damaged ankle, and he had all the next day to cover the fifteen miles to the river, so he took off his shoes and soaked his ankles and feet in the cold water. The ankle had begun to swell, but now it felt mostly numb, and the swelling had ceased. For half an hour he alternately soaked and massaged, and by sundown his ankle was feeling better. Nothing was broken, and he hoped that by morning he could walk without pain. He crossed the creek on a fallen log, found a secluded place behind a pile of brush, opened his pack and ate biscuits and dried meat. He rolled out his blanket and went to sleep.

He was awake again before dawn. He rose and tested his ankle, which was stiff but seemed much improved. He ate a little more food and took a long drink, refilled the canteen from the creek, secured and shouldered his possessions and began to walk. He took his time, up a long rise for three miles or so, down again for a couple of miles, across a smaller spring-fed creek. Again he drank the contents of his canteen, refilled it, and had another mouthful of food, then started up another rise. By now he figured he might be half way. He was moving slowly, taking it as easy as possible on the injured leg. The sun was not yet overhead, so he had plenty of time.

From the top of this rise he saw in the distance a long string of low hills covered with dark trees, likely blackjacks, the scrubby oak that he'd found common downriver in eighty-nine. From here the land was mostly flat, easy walking through short grass prairie and here and there patches of wheat. He walked parallel to the trail, sometimes in the roadway, which was crowded and dusty with walkers and horses and wagons, but more often in the solitude of the prairie.

By early afternoon he came to the tiny settlement of Lacey, a few crude houses and a general store. It was still raw, being just a couple of years old. He stopped and inquired about what lay ahead. The proprietor was a talkative fellow, answering questions that Reuben didn't have. Whether he was hoping to establish friendly relations with potential new customers, or simply liked to talk, Reuben couldn't tell. He told Reuben the place was named for John F. Lacey, a congressman from Iowa. More important to Reuben at the moment was that he had only five miles to go.

From Lacey, Reuben veered southwest. Most people were following the trail straight west, and the map in Reuben's head had the river angling southeast, so there were two reasons for his course. A southwesterly route should be perpendicular to the river, and thus the shortest distance, but more important, he hoped to escape much of the crowd. In a couple of miles he entered the region of sand dunes he'd seen from miles back, densely covered with blackjacks and brush. He fought his way through tangles and brambles, arriving at a summit from which he could see across more low dunes, and then a valley of tall native grasses to the wooded course that must be the Cimarron. He descended to the river bottom. The sand was loose, obviously former river bed. It grew grasses, flowering broad-leafed plants and sage brush. Searching the horizon, Reuben picked out one steep rise on the opposite bank. Perhaps a place that a rider on horseback could not ascend, but a man on foot might scale. He directed his steps toward that bluff.

When he arrived the sun was low in the west, but the air was still warm. If he'd hoped for solitude, he'd been wrong. A throng of people, horses and wagons lined the river's edge. Every spot along the water was taken. He chose a place near a thicket of willows, fifty feet from the bank. He ate and drank again, took off his shoes and massaged his still swollen ankle, sprawled on the sand with his bundle for a pillow and went to sleep. Tomorrow he hoped would be the culmination of his dreams. But he also knew it might be his last chance to gain a quarter section of free Indian land.

CHAPTER 5

"Wichita," Arden Breedlove said. He pulled a roll of bills from his pocket and the agent handed him a ticket. The agent recognized him, of course, but Arden had been to Wichita on official business before, so no questions were asked. Arden glanced down the line behind him. Nobody he knew. He pulled his cap low over his eyes, grasped his bag and headed for the train.

Getting to or out of Fort Scott had been much more difficult when he'd arrived on foot during the Civil War. The Missouri River Fort Scott & Gulf Railroad had put Fort Scott on the map in September of 1869 as something more than a good place to fight and die. Over the years Fort Scott had become a booming town, and he'd had a part in that. Actually, two parts. Not only had he helped extend the railroad between there and Wichita on which he now would ride, but for more than a decade he'd served as an officer of the peace in the frontier town. But that was before last night.

It was mostly luck that he'd given them the slip. He had tiptoed back into the house, looked long upon his sleeping wife, gathered clothes, food and everything else he'd need for the journey and packed it in a big leather bag. He put on a clean uniform, strapped his service revolver to his belt, stuffed the bloody uniform into a gunny sack and crept out the door. He walked to a ravine at the edge of town and set the gunny sack on fire. He carried his bag through deserted streets and hid it in a woodpile behind the depot. Then he resumed his beat, walking the downtown streets until dawn.

When his shift was over he had breakfast at the hotel and took money out of the bank. He intended to withdraw it all, but as he approached the teller he realized that might draw suspicion. He took half and left the rest for Maggie. Then, just in case somebody found the body, he hid in an abandoned warehouse by the railroad tracks. He changed from his uniform to dungarees and a flannel shirt, stashed the uniform under a pile of boxes, and snuggled the revolver into the clothing in his bag. He watched through a grimy window until the sun was setting. The train would take him to the big city by the next dawn.

The conductor blew his whistle and the doors slammed shut. There were few empty seats. Most were occupied by men traveling light, like himself. There were the usual businessmen in suits, a family or two with passels of kids, but mostly it was single men of a rougher sort. After a decade as a cop he could pick a hustler from a block away, and there were plenty of those, men who would soon pull out a bottle of whisky and a deck of cards and try to stir up a game with some country hick, of which there were also plenty. Maybe some were headed to Wichita in search of a job, but who knew where so many yokels might be going?

Breedlove pulled his cap even lower, rolled a cigarette and stared out the window as the train rolled through fading lights past the cattle yards and the long stretch of shacks and onto the open prairie and fields. The chatter picked up as darkness fell. Men jostled and jabbered, smoked and played cards by the light of flickering lamps. Mothers huddled with children, trying to shield them from the swearing and swagger of fellow travelers. The man in the next seat tried to strike up a conversation, but Breedlove cut him off with a cold glance and a grunt. He snuffed out his smoke and closed his eyes.

It was unlike him to act without a plan. Starting the day he walked away from the farm at sixteen and joined the Rebel army, he had mostly acted deliberately. There were two kinds of people, the ones who made the rules and those who suffered by them, the ones who planned their next move and those whose next moves were decided by others, the winners who looked out for themselves and those who lost the game. Men who merely floated with the current never got ahead.

It had never been easy staying ahead of the game. When you're one of half a dozen kids on a hilly sixty-acre farm in the west Missouri hills, there's little to make you hang around. Then along comes the fight over slavery, and the old man joins up with what some people called the border ruffians, not because he had slaves, which he was far too poor to own, but because he detested both black people and white people rich enough to own them, and because every time he disappeared across the Kansas line for a few days on what he called a mission, he came home with a pocketful of cash.

When Arden was thirteen the southern states seceded from the Union. The Civil War began in April, and nothing was normal anymore. Many neighbors, especially the younger men, joined one army or the other, and some who stayed at home took advantage of the chaos to settle old scores, to rob and terrorize neighbors, even to run a family of women and kids out of their home and grab their farm. So alongside the official battles of the bigger war, there were the raids and skirmishes of gangs on both sides of the border. The anti-slavery folks in Kansas had their own guerrilla bushwhackers, the Jayhawkers. It was this gang that sacked the Breedloves' closest town, Osceola, in September.

Osceola was a booming town of three thousand mostly pro-South people built on the Osage River after the Osage Indians were pushed out to Kansas. It somehow got named for a Seminole chief who fought federal soldiers in the Florida Everglades. Arden knew little about Osceola the Indian—he'd heard that Osceola was captured and died a prisoner of war—and not much about the town, but he knew it better than any other; in fact it was the only town he had ever seen. It was a five mile walk from the Breedlove farm, so visits were rare. Just the same, when the Jayhawkers burned Osceola to the ground it solidified a hatred in young Arden that he had not previously known. He tried to join the rebel army then, but they wouldn't take a thirteen-year-old kid.

For awhile Arden's father stayed to fight off the Jayhawkers and bushwhackers, but increasingly he would disappear when the sun went down, leaving Arden and his older brother to take care of their mother and the farm. Some said his father's band of border ruffians were now little more than bushwhackers themselves, with little allegiance to either side. What followed was three years of chaos and fear, of battles fought all over the countryside, of rotting away on the farm, watching out for thugs, trying to help his mother keep the family fed, waiting for something else to happen. Then in September of 1864, the day he turned sixteen, Arden walked into what was left of Osceola and put on the Confederate uniform.

His career as a soldier was brief, not because the war soon came to an end, but because in his first skirmish, the Battle of Marmiton River on October 25, his face was slashed by a musket ball. When he came to he found himself in a chaotic field of carnage, gray men and blue men sprawled as they fell, distorted limbs, blood, the shrieks and wailing of the not-yet dead. A dead man's arm draped across his chest. He cried out in horror, flung off the embrace and struggled to his knees. He dragged a sleeve across his bloody face. His gray uniform was dark with mud and blood.

Arden staggered to his feet. He picked up his musket, filled his canteen from the canteens of the fallen, gathered bits of food, filled his pockets with powder and lead and gazed to the west. The blood-red sky mirrored the battle scene. He walked to the river and washed his face and hands. The deep gash continued to seep. He tied a bandana around his head and across the wound, ate and drank, and staggered toward the dying sun.

At daylight he crawled into a tangle of dogwood and sumac and slept. When the sun was high, he awoke and saw a farmhouse near. A woman was taking clothes off a line. He followed a shallow swale to the edge of the yard and waited for the woman to take a basket of dried clothes into the house. He climbed the fence, took a shirt and overalls and two clean bandanas off the line, took them to the barn and put them on. Leaving the uniform behind, he walked out the driveway to the road and continued west.

If it had not been for the gaping wound on his cheek, passage might have been easy. A sixteen year old would not necessarily be taken for a soldier—or a deserter. But with the bandana tied around his face he thought it best to avoid encounters. For two days he traveled mostly by night and by country lanes, taking food as he found it. Finally he came to the Kansas line.

He first saw the lights of Fort Scott in the middle of the night, off to the southwest, and turned his feet that way. He arrived on the edge of town at dawn, and as luck would have it, a woman had just emerged from the first house he passed and was pumping water at the well. He was very hungry, and decided to take a chance. He hid his musket in some weeds and approached.

"Good morning, Ma'am," he said. "I was just wondering if you could spare a piece of bread. I was attacked by bushwhackers over in Missouri and I've been walking for days to get away."

At first the woman was alarmed, perhaps by the bloody bandage across his cheek. But she saw that he was a young lad in need, and he seemed harmless enough. "Yes, of course I can give you breakfast," she said. She led him into the house. "But first let's take a look at that wound." She set him down by a kitchen window and removed the bandage. She sucked through her teeth when she saw the still-raw cut. "How did that happen?" she asked.

"They slashed me with a hatchet," he said. "Lucky I'm a fast runner, and I got away."

The woman poured water into a pan and shook in a few drops of iodine. She took a clean cloth from a drawer and bathed the wound, then dressed it with a proper bandage that looked less shocking to the eye. Then she put bacon in a skillet and cooked Arden the first real meal he had eaten in days.

As he ate he realized it was also the first kindness he had experienced in a very long time. Perhaps there were still good people in the world. He thanked her for all she had done and started for town. When she had gone back inside he went back to the weed patch and retrieved his rifle. Then, avoiding the town, he walked on west.

Thus began a looping journey that took Arden Breedlove through more than a decade and the American West. He herded cattle on a western Kansas ranch, drove an ox team on a supply wagon as far as the Willamette Valley on the Oregon Trail, broke horses on a ranch west of the Black Hills until an untamed paint threw him and broke his ankle. There was no doctor to properly set the bone, and when he could finally walk again, it was with a limp that he would always carry. Besides that he was tired of wandering, of living hand to mouth. So in 1880 he worked his way back toward home. He returned to the farm outside Osceola, only to find the house burned to the foundation, his family gone. He inquired in town and learned that his father and older brother were dead. His mother and the younger kids had disappeared, gone back to east Tennessee where she had relatives, a neighbor said. Arden caught the train for Fort Scott.

He knew nobody in Fort Scott. He'd heard all the stories, of course. Everybody had. The Army had abandoned the old frontier fort in 1853, just as the battle between pro-slavery and abolitionist forces was heating up. Congress passed the Kansas-Nebraska Act the next year, which opened the territory to legal settlement. People of every stripe flooded across the line into the new territory, most for free land, others to advance the fight over whether the future state would be slave or free. Violence broke out everywhere in what came to be known as "bleeding Kansas."

There were the well-known stories, like the one about abolitionist John Brown and his followers murdering pro-slavers, or the gang of slave-owning settlers from South Carolina that terrorized and drove out settlers opposed to slavery. But that was the tip of the iceberg. Hearing these tales as a boy, Arden never imagined he would come to a place he associated with such violence and fear. That, of course, was before the same fates visited Osceola, and eventually the families and farms he knew. So he had long since come to terms with fear and set it aside. What would happen would happen, but you would be foolish to turn your back.

He walked to the northern outskirts, but couldn't locate the house where the woman had given him breakfast and care. He wandered the town until he saw a notice posted on the depot door. The Saint Louis, Fort Scott, Wichita and Western Railroad had been chartered to extend the railroad to Wichita, and there were jobs to be had. He applied, and went to work on a crew bedding ties and driving spikes. The work was hard, the pay low. Not the kind of future he'd gradually come to hope for. He was thirty-two and had no more to show for himself than when he walked away from the farm at half that age. He worked the line through the summer and fall, but when the weather grew cold he rode the supply train back to Fort Scott. He walked to the hotel for the first good dinner he'd had in weeks. Inside the door he saw a notice that veterans were being recruited for the town's police force.

Next morning Breedlove visited a barber shop for a haircut and shave, bought a new set of clothes and went to city hall to apply. He did not report that he was a deserter from the Confederate Army. Instead he had served honorably as a Union soldier. He mentioned the still vivid scar on his cheek and the crooked ankle, described the Union victory at the Battle of Marmiton River in which he was wounded, and got the job.

At last he felt he had found the right road. He was treated with respect, or fear, and it didn't much matter which. Even young women smiled at him in his uniform, especially a young woman who waitressed at the hotel. Her name was Maggie. She was nineteen, a pretty girl who like him had come in from the farm. At dinner one night he asked her to go to a vaudeville show when she got off work, and she agreed. They dated for a few months, and in the spring they were married before the justice of the peace. Life was good for awhile, but gradually things began to unravel.

Now the train window was black, a mirror that reflected his own scarred face in need of a shave and those of fellow travelers. His seatmate had gone to sleep. The rhythm of the wheels clicking across the expansion joints was soothing, and he closed his eyes. When he did he saw Maggie's face. What would become of her now, he wondered. She had wanted babies, and if they had come, things might have turned out differently. The night shift paid better, so that was what he'd generally worked, but that kept them apart. Maybe that was a mistake.

And it certainly wasn't all her fault. There were lots of temptations for a cop in a raw town like Fort Scott, and temptations were greatest on the night shift: the backrooms where dice were rolled and cards were played and where he gained skill in those games and often won, the sensual pleasures at the Diamond T, and sometimes money offered under the table to look the other way.

Across the Cimarron

CHAPTER 6

Maybe it was handed down from his father, but for whatever reason, Arden Breedlove couldn't get over a grudge. Take the Jayhawkers, for example. Maybe they were no worse than ruffians like his father, and who knows which side was more brutal or wrong in the war, but it was the Jayhawkers who'd burned his town in sixty-one, and now he lived in the Jayhawker's nest. After a decade the town was a mix, of course, plenty of veterans from both sides, including men with far worse wounds than his—men missing arms or legs or eyes, crazed men who lay drunk behind the saloon.

There were still a few old abolitionists who thought Negroes should be treated like whites, plenty of former slave holders for whom nothing had really changed, even a few black people huddled in shacks on the edge of town. He tried to rise above it all, tried to ignore the conflicts and stay out of fights. But there were plenty of people with a chip on their shoulders against cops, especially the old pro-slavery crowd who thought he'd fought for the Union side.

But with the Brady boys, it was more personal, especially when he found out that after his father died and his mother was desperate to feed the younger kids, the Bradys' uncle had swindled her out of the deed to the Breedlove farm.

Maybe the nephews had nothing to do with it, but they were an inescapable reminder, and once when he was drunk, Lloyd even tried to rub it in. "Why don't you go back to the farm?" he taunted. "I happen to know the folks who own it now, and maybe I could get you a job cleaning out the barn."

Beyond his general aversion to the Bradys, he wasn't sure what had made him suspicious when Lloyd and Davis stopped him outside the Diamond T and tried to lure him in to meet the new girl. He was sure that his dislike for them was mutual; they weren't likely to take an interest in his welfare—or his pleasure. "She's just arrived from New Orleans," Lloyd said, "a hot little number, and she wants to make friends with the local authorities."

"I'm on duty tonight, you know that," he said. "I have rounds to make."

"Oh come on," Davis said. "If you don't feel like a tumble tonight, at least you have time for a game of cards, unless, of course, you're scared we'll take your money."

"That's not likely," Arden replied. "You might recall how it turned out last time we played. By the way, where's big brother? The three of you always look for trouble together. Aren't you afraid to be out at night without big Bob?"

He turned his back and resumed his pace up the boardwalk. He seethed inside, just from being in the presence of the Brady boys. Not only did it bring back bad memories, and not only was it likely that they had some trick up their sleeves, but they had taken every opportunity to rub him the wrong way ever since the night he'd thrown Bob in the tank for a drunken fight at the hotel.

"Well, if you're scared to hang around with us low-life Rebels, that's OK," Davis called after him. "You know how yellow Yankees are," he said to his brother. "Especially Yankee cops."

Arden didn't look back. It was bad enough being called a coward, or a Yankee if you were one, but even worse if you weren't but everybody thought you were. But he had beat these yokels at their own game before, and he was sure he could do it again. He spat on the street and ignored the taunt.

Yet he couldn't get Bob Brady out of his head. He remembered something Brady had said the morning they let him out of jail, something about Arden's wife. It was only the uniform he wore that had stopped him from smashing Brady's face, and then just barely. But what if there was something to it? Unlike his brothers, Bob did have a certain reputation as a lady's man. Why, Arden had no idea.

He had never suspected Maggie would step out of line, and certainly not with a low life like a Bob Brady, but pausing under the street lamp he looked back toward the Diamond T. The sidewalk was empty. Lloyd and Davis had gone back inside. But why wasn't Bob with them like always?

Arden was headed north anyway, so he kept walking. When he got to his house, the lights were out as they should be. Nothing seemed amiss. He paused by the gate post and rolled a cigarette. He thought of going in and checking whether Maggie was awake. They hadn't slept together for a week, and it might be nice. He lighted the cigarette and inhaled.

The night was calm and he thought he heard a noise inside. He listened carefully, and he heard it again. There was a man's voice. He opened the gate and crept close to the bedroom window. There were murmurs inside. He couldn't make out the words, but then he heard Maggie laugh. He snuffed out the cigarette and waited.

He fingered his gun, wondering whether to go in or wait. Moments passed, and the back door squeaked open. In the starlight Breedlove saw the big-belly profile of Bob Brady. Brady stood on the porch, adjusted his belt and gazed up at the stars, then stepped down and ambled down the garden path toward the alley.

What should he do? Should he shoot Brady in the back? He would be within his rights. Or maybe it was Maggie he should kill, or maybe both? It took a moment for the reality to sink in. He couldn't believe that Maggie would do that to him, especially with scum like a Brady. And it was even harder to believe that Bob Brady would have the nerve.

Now Brady was out the gate and disappearing in the shadows. Should he follow him down the alley? Wait and confront him in the street? Go in and take care of Maggie and deal with Brady later? He couldn't call the law, because he was the law. There were laws of course, but what proof would he have? Anyway, what man would stand the disgrace of publicly admitting that his wife had taken his antagonist to bed? There was only one way to handle it. He would deal with Maggie later. He turned back toward Main Street, where sooner or later Bob Brady would appear.

He hadn't long to wait. Brady emerged from the darkness of the alley at the first corner. "Bob Brady, you foul skunk son of a bitch, I know where you've been, and now I know where you're going!" he called. His Remington was in his hand.

Brady froze in his tracks and turned. In the dim light that reached from the lamp posts downtown he recognized Breedlove, likely saw the gun in his hand. "I don't know what you're talking about," he stammered. Breedlove was advancing, and now they were twenty paces apart. Breedlove saw Brady reach behind his belt. The policeman's revolver exploded and the big man went to the ground. Breedlove paced toward Brady, his pistol trained on the other's head.

Brady was on his back, blood seeping from his chest. His arms inched away from his body and above his head. "Don't kill me, Arden," he whimpered. "I've got nothing against you. And you've got nothing on me."

"The hell I don't," Breedlove said. "I should've shot you the day we let you out of jail. But better late than never. I ought to kill you for fooling with my wife. But I think I'll do it out of general principal instead, just because I don't like you, just because you aren't fit to live." He pulled the trigger again. Brady flinched once and was quiet.

Dogs were barking all over the north side of town. In a window across the street a lamp was lighted. The front door opened and a man poked out his head. Arden didn't move, waiting for the door to close. When It did, he grasped Brady's bloody shoulders and strained to drag him back toward the alley. He remembered that behind the Campbell house there was a jungle of lilac bushes. When he arrived with his burden he dragged and shoved until the heavy body was deposited in the middle of the shrubs. He gathered brush and covered the corpse. He wiped his hands on the grass and stood. Nobody about. He ought to get out of town, but it was just past midnight, and the next train didn't leave until evening. Should he go for his horse, clean up and go back to work, or find a place to hide? For a man who tried to plan his moves a step ahead, Arden Breedlove was suddenly at a loss.

He could go home and take care of Maggie, one way or the other. But he'd already killed one; maybe that was enough. And in truth, maybe Arden shouldn't have been surprised. He knew he hadn't satisfied her, that she wanted what he couldn't give her, and maybe he even had it coming since he'd fooled around too, and likely she knew about that.

No, it would do no good to kill Maggie, even if he wanted to, and he didn't want to. He still loved her, but whatever had been between them had to be over now. It was like the day he'd walked out the driveway at sixteen. It was time to move on. That left just one thing to do, and that wasn't hanging around Fort Scott to face a jury or a judge. Justice had been done. It was time for a new chapter, one he hadn't planned.

Across the Cimarron

CHAPTER 7

The eastern sky was pink when the train dragged into the station in Wichita. Breedlove picked up his bag and stepped off. The platform was a gaggle of men, jostling for position to meet the other men getting off the train. Amidst the din, certain phrases rang out: ride to Oklahoma Territory, free land, make the run. He'd heard vaguely about the new land opening, Indian land west of the Cimarron. On the train he'd perked up his ears and listened to voices, some low and conspiratorial, others boastful and loud, but weaving together scraps the picture had emerged— the latest, and maybe the best or last run for free land in Oklahoma Territory was about to begin, land that apparently the government had acquired from the Cheyenne and Arapaho tribes.

He elbowed his way through the crowd, ignoring offers of guides, wagons and teams, promises of choice places speculators had mapped. Inside the depot he found an official notice tacked on the wall, along with a map of the vast region to be opened, from the Cherokee Outlet south to the Canadian River and west from the Cimarron to the Texas line. The notice said the Indians had already been assigned allotments, and three and a half million acres were up for grabs, one hundred and sixty acres a whack. The run was scheduled for noon, April 19.

That was two days away! What luck. It almost made him believe what he'd heard a preacher say once, that when one door closes another will open up. He'd had enough of the farm; from his family's experience back in Missouri, a farm was a good place to either starve or work yourself to death, or both. But the newspaper speculated that 25,000 people would make the run, and not everybody would get a place, at least not choice farm land. If he could get a piece of land it would sooner or later be worth money, and in the meantime, nobody would be looking for him in the middle of nowhere.

He studied the map. A train ran south all the way to the Canadian River, so he could ride it to Hennessey. From there it looked like about fifteen miles west to the Cimarron. It was good he'd fled Fort Scott by train instead of on horseback, not only because the get-away was faster, but by horse there was no way he could have arrived in time. On the other hand, once he got to Hennessey he'd need transportation to the river and some way to make the run. He'd need to find another a horse.

The next southbound train was scheduled for ten o'clock. Breedlove stepped to the ticket window. "Sorry, if you were thinking of taking the train today you're out of luck," the agent said without looking up from papers he was checking. "I might be able to get you on tomorrow."

"I need a ticket today," Breedlove said. "I aim to be in Hennessey this afternoon."

The agent looked up from his work. "As I said, today's train is full. There's nothing I can do."

Breedlove pulled his roll of bills from his pocket. "However much the ticket is, I'm paying double," he said. "The extra is for you."

"Well," the agent said, eyeing Breedlove over his spectacles, "In that case, maybe there's something I can do." He reached under the counter and pulled out a roll of tickets and tore one free. Breedlove handed the man a ten dollar bill and collected his ticket and a handful of change. He had time for a big breakfast and took his seat on the train.

For six hours the train rolled south, stopping in raw little towns to take on water and coal and to let off the few passengers who weren't bound for the promised land. When it screeched to a halt in Hennessey, the sun was still high above the horizon. Breedlove swung his bag over his shoulder and strode toward the livery barn.

Trying to buy a horse in Hennessey was worse than buying a ticket in Wichita. He wasn't the only man with that plan. He looked over the half dozen or so nags in the stalls. A couple were so old and sway backed he doubted they would go the distance, at least not at the speed he'd need. There was a giddy gelding that obviously wasn't broke, a couple of mares and a big roan stallion. Breedlove eyed the roan. It was tall, long strong legs. Its teeth showed it to be not more than five years old. He couldn't tell if he saw meanness, wildness or just spirit in its eyes. Spirit was good, and wildness might also be good for frontier life. If it was meanness, he knew how to handle that. He was no expert in horses, but this one looked like it could run, like it could still be running when most horses were done. "How much for the roan?" he asked.

The livery man chuckled. "Oh, I doubt you could afford that boy," he said. "I could give you a deal on a good mare."

"I want the roan," Breedlove said. "What's your price?"

"Whew," the other man said. "You must be loaded. This horse won't come cheap."

"How much?" Breedlove repeated. His unflinching stare broke the other's gaze.

"Well, if you're set on the stallion, it will set you back fifty dollars."

"Fifty dollars! Man you are no horse dealer. You're a horse thief's nightmare. I'll give you twenty and not back out."

The other man laughed long and loud. "Maybe you can find an old plow horse from some farmer outside town," he said when his laughing died. "Fifty dollars is the price."

Breedlove pulled a half-smoked cigar from his pocket and bit it in his teeth. He peeled back the stallion's lips and looked him over for some imperfection he could name. There was a scar on a foreleg, but that wouldn't slow the big boy down—or make him less virile when it came to breeding mares. For the first time Breedlove saw the roan not only as a means of transportation, but as a stud, as an important asset for a businessman in a new territory. There would be plenty of farmers across the river with mares to breed, and whatever he paid for the stallion, he was bound to recoup his investment in time.

"Let me ask you a question," Breedlove said. "Are you a card-playing man?"

"Sure, I guess so," the other replied. "Why do you ask?"

"Tell you what. Let's play a hand of poker. If you win, I'll pay your price for the horse. If I win, I'll give you twenty-five."

The liveryman pursed his lips and thought a moment. He eyed Breedlove from head to toe, pausing too long on the nasty scar, trying to decide whether Breedlove was just a crazy gambler, or maybe a shark. "OK," he said at last. "You've got yourself a deal."

The pair sat down on two bales of hay with another bale between. Breedlove handed a deck of cards to the horseman. "Here, you deal," he said. "That way you'll be sure the game is fair."

The liveryman shuffled the cards, Arden cut them, and the other dealt. The dealer looked over his cards and arranged them. A broad smile spread across his face. "Looks like you just bought yourself an expensive horse," he said. "How does three jacks sound?" He laid his cards on the bale.

"Not a bad hand," Arden replied. "But where I come from it won't beat a straight." Arden laid out his cards one by one, a three, a four, a five, a six and a seven of spades. "And you can keep the cards for a souvenir," he added. He pulled out his wallet and counted out two tens and a five—about what he figured a good horse was worth under normal circumstances, though present circumstances were far from normal. He paid the gaping liveryman another five for a well-worn saddle and bridle, led the stallion to the general store, tied him to the rail and went in for supplies.

Arden came out with bacon, potatoes, beans, dried beef, biscuits, salt and coffee in a burlap bag. He cinched this and his satchel behind the saddle and turned the horse west. The trail, if you could call it that, was jammed with wagons and buckboards and horses, even families trudging west in the cloud of dust. Arden avoided the cluttered trail, keeping his horse in the grassy roadside. When he gave him the reins it was clear that the stallion was ready to run, but Arden reined him in, moving at a steady pace down the bluff, across a creek and a plain, through a blackjack ridge and past the settlement of Lacey, on through another ridge of sand dunes and blackjacks to where the prairie opened to the Cimarron. Running he would save for tomorrow.

Arden rode to the top of the highest dune, where the sand was so loose the stallion's hooves sank deep, where the waving prairie grasses were replaced by mostly sage brush and soap weeds. From this promontory he scanned the river bottom for miles, and the rising bluff on the other side. A long stretch of the Cimarron and the thousands of people and horses and wagons and makeshift tents were obscured by a hovering cloud of dust. He saw that to the far south of where the primitive road would meet the river, a long island separated two channels, widening the river to perhaps a quarter mile. There the encampment thinned, and there also a wide ravine ran to the river from the west.

When he reached the river, the sun had set. Arden turned south, surveying the crowd and sizing up the competition, looking particularly for horses that might compete with the roan. He rode into a thick grove of cottonwoods and hackberries, where he was hidden from the crowd. He dug in his heals, and the big horse plunged into the river, wading and loping until the water was deep, then swimming easily across the current until his hooves again touched sand, then scrambling up the bank. Breedlove rode south toward the ravine and across a creek. Again he slammed his heels into the flanks and the roan galloped up the sloping bluff.

On top Breedlove rode south along the bluff a mile or so, then turned and rode back across the creek and up the bluff the other way, staying away from the edge so he would not be visible from across the river. Darkness was falling when he found a quarter he liked just north of the ravine, a place with a fresh water spring. He dismounted, and both man and horse drank of the cool, sweet water. He gazed back across the river at the milling crowd, now dimly lighted by flickering fires. There were hundreds of teams and wagons, loaded with everything a family owned. More numerous were the milling men, thousands of them, some with horses, a few without. Those with wagons and those on foot were no threat, and from what he'd seen so far of his twenty-five dollar stallion, it was unlikely there were many who wouldn't be eating his dust.

Breedlove turned in the saddle and gazed west. Free land stretched for a hundred miles, but it was likely that land by the river—and nearer to what passed for civilization—would bring the highest price in a year or two. So this was the place. He turned the horse back toward the ravine, down the bluff to the river and across. He dismounted and watered his horse again, then tied the reins to a willow sapling, a temporary claim on a scrap of sandbar twenty paces from the water, a good jumping off spot for the race.

CHAPTER 8

The aroma of cooking meat was in the air, and Arden wished he'd bought a piece of fresh beef to roast. For now he would have to be satisfied with jerky and biscuits. He gathered driftwood and made a small fire. There were bound to be deer and other animals to hunt along the river, so fresh meat would come. Munching the dry food and washing it down with water from the spring he'd found, he surveyed his neighbors. There was a woman with a wagon and kids, apparently no man. He thought of Maggie. Maybe he should have brought her, but he was pretty sure she wouldn't have wanted to come. Or maybe he would even go back for her once he'd settled in. Settled in? Here he was thinking like these other yokels who thought that just because they had a piece of Indian land, they could make a go of it here. He knew better. His family had never gotten far beyond hand to mouth on the Missouri farm, and across the river the land looked hard. If the size of the Cimarron was any indication, the territory probably got little rain.

He tried not to think about Maggie, or about the man he'd killed. He wanted to focus on tomorrow, on fulfilling his emerging plan, on getting a river bluff farm with fresh water that sooner or later would sell for a good price. But gazing into the flickering flames, the images of the past two days were hard to squelch. He wondered what Maggie was doing now. One thing was sure, she wasn't in bed with Bob Brady! Had they found the body yet? Since Arden didn't show up for work it probably wouldn't take even the dim-witted so-called detectives on the force long to figure out what happened. Even Lloyd and Davis would put two and two together. So by now there was probably a warrant out for his arrest, and maybe a posse. He was confident they'd never look for him here, but going back for Maggie, or even trying to get in touch would be risky. The red had faded in the west, and a chilly breeze blew down the river. He huddled closer to the fire, remembering Maggie's warmth in their early days together. But he had to stop thinking about what he'd left behind.

A baby cried, and a Negro man emerged from a canvas hovel. He approached a man who hunched under a blanket to his south and asked for medicine. Arden thought he'd left them behind in Missouri and Kansas, but apparently not. He couldn't believe the government would let coloreds compete with whites as if they were equals in this race for free land. "Knock off the chatter, darkie," Arden barked. "I can't believe they're lettin you niggers run anyhow. There's more hard-workin white men than there is land, folks that can make something out of this." The Negro quoted something from the Bible and went back to his lean-to.

Arden knew his fire of willows and driftwood would not last long, so he pulled out his blanket and rolled it around him and lay down on the sand. In spite of the smoke from so many smoldering fires, the sky was brilliant with a million stars. He realized that he hadn't lain down under a sky like this for years, not since he came back from the West. In Fort Scott the nights were rarely this clear, and in town the darkness was compromised by street lamps. He knew he had no intention to stay permanently on the land he would take tomorrow, but he did feel nostalgic for the freedom and openness, for the uncluttered beauty he remembered from his decade of roaming.

When Arden awoke the eastern sky was rosy. He was amazed that he'd slept so well on the cold, damp sand. All along the Cimarron people were stirring, building up fires, frying bacon. How much would he give for a big hot breakfast of bacon and eggs and grits? Why hadn't he taken time in Wichita, or even Hennessey, to lay in some real food, not just something to keep him alive? It might be a long time until he could find a good meal again, and at what price? At least he'd brought coffee. He rebuilt his fire, poured water in a pot and boiled hot dark coffee to wash down his barely palatable food.

It would be a long wait until noon. He almost wished he'd simply hid out in a ravine on the other side. He was sure that others had done so. He'd heard that men called Boomers, or Sooners, or something of the like, had been infiltrating the territory for months, ready to pounce on choice land they'd already picked. But likely there were soldiers patrolling somewhere on the other side, and if he were caught he'd be out of the race.

To Arden's south was the man the Negro had asked for medicine. The poor bum didn't even have a horse. He apparently thought he could actually compete on foot. There were others like him too. He knew the odds hadn't always favored him either, but at least he was realistic. He had to chuckle at people who were either too dumb or too down and out, or maybe just desperate, that they thought they could somehow get a farm without being prepared. Of course the land did run for a hundred miles or more—all the way to the Texas Panhandle the map said —so theoretically a man could walk for days until he finally found land that was beyond what anybody else wanted.

The morning dragged on, but finally the sun neared its zenith, and activity along the river's edge reached a fever pitch. People checked and rechecked wagon wheels and lines, cinched bundles tighter, gave nervous orders to kids. Arden himself shifted and retied the bundle he'd strapped behind the saddle, rechecked the stallion's hooves and waited. Then a thought occurred to him. He'd had this horse for nearly two days and still hadn't given him a name. What should he be called? "Well," he said to the roan, "you're gonna be first out of the blocks and we will be first across the river, first to the top, first to drive a stake. So I'll call you Boomer. Boomer it is. Are you ready boy?"

Arden mounted his steed and waited. A man climbed up on a wagon box and waived his hands for quiet, which of course didn't happen. He tried to explain the rules of the run over the din, then raised his arm high and fired. Arden dug his heels deep into Boomer's flanks and the horse leapt into action, across the sand bar, into the water, swimming fast, dancing through quicksand on the west bank, then through tangles of brush, and finally free, galloping at full stride south toward the gash in the bluff a mile away. The horse and rider were not alone; there were countless other "boomers" in the fray, ridden by men as self-assured as

Arden, likewise bent on the easy ascent offered by the gully cut by the entering stream, equally determined to be first on top. One horse stumbled in front of Arden and its rider tumbled headlong through a tangle of brush. Two others were ahead, and Arden whipped Boomer again and again, urging him on. They passed one rider as they entered the ravine, and the other horse splashed across the creek and headed south. Now Arden was in the lead, scrambling up the north bank. When they reached the top Boomer was winded, but Arden pushed him on, streaking across the bluff toward the pile of rocks he'd found the evening before.

Suddenly a man appeared at the edge of the bluff, grasping branches and bushes hand over hand, then dragging himself over the top. The man leapt to his feet, sprinted to the marker and pulled a stake from his pack. That was Arden's quarter! He couldn't believe it possible that some fool on foot had gotten there first. And now there would be a confrontation and he'd left the Remington in his bag. Now the man was coming into better focus. Strangely enough, instead of driving in his stake the man crouched on his knees, holding a rock in his hands. But then the man set that rock aside, chose another and brought it down, driving the stake into the ground. Then he pulled a revolver from his belt and aimed it straight at Arden.

Arden reined Boomer in, in a cloud of dust. The man who had stolen his claim was the dumb farmer he'd camped beside, the man on foot, who was now threatening to kill him. What could he do? There was no way to go for his own gun. He memorized the man's face. He was sure they would meet again. He dug in his heels and Boomer charged on west, past the sweet spring, onto treeless higher plains. The sandy land of the eastern bank had turned to red. "Hard land," Arden muttered. "But at least it's not full of rocks like Missouri. Ought to grow corn." Maybe somebody would pay good money for such a farm.

At last Boomer could run no more and settled to a snorting trot, sweat flying from his neck. They were maybe three or four miles from the river, and judging by the cloud of dust, they'd left the mob of wagons a good mile behind. Arden focused on the lay of the land. He mounted a little rise, and before him lay a long stretch of prairie grasses and flowers that sloped just right. Across the southeast corner a strip of trees indicated a meandering stream. He found the marker, dismounted and drove his stake.

Across the Cimarron

CHAPTER 9

When Boomer was rested, Arden mounted and rode the perimeters of the quarter section he had claimed. Here and there he slid down and kicked up scraps of sod with his boot. The grass was heavy and thick—buffalo grass, blue stem, others he didn't recognize, dotted here and there with blooming broadleaf plants, yellows, reds, whites, even blue. The soil seemed pretty good, hard but undoubtedly rich to have grown such luxuriant grass. But for April, the soil seemed dry. Near the trickling creek he found a dried elm branch and dug down several inches to where the moisture disappeared altogether and he could dig no deeper. No wonder the thousands of hooves and wagon wheels had kicked up so much dust.

He found the source of the little creek, not much more than a seep. He led Boomer to the water, and he drank deep and long. Arden squatted upstream, cupped his hands and drank. The water tasted of minerals, perhaps gypsum, not sweet like the spring that damned farmer had beat him to. If this was the flow in April, would it still be running in August? He boiled at the thought of the man who had beat him to his intended land, land with an abundant spring. He'd already killed one man this week. If only he'd had the Remington in his hand.

What was he thinking? Yes, he had killed another man. It was never his intention, it just happened that way. And now he was thinking he should have killed again? What had he become? Here he had gained a chance to leave the past behind, to start anew. He'd have to make the most of the opportunity, one way or another, and killing another man would not be a good way to start. And yet he couldn't get that dirt-scratcher out of his mind,

61

especially the fact that after taunting him about making the run on foot the guy had actually beat him at the game. He didn't like to lose. Yes, someday they would meet again.

Arden gathered a few fallen branches and made a little lean-to against a low horizontal limb. He pulled a canvas tarp from his bag and stretched it across to form a roof, something that would shed water if rain should come. That didn't look likely; the sky was unadulterated blue. He gathered more sticks so that when night fell he could have a fire. He unsaddled Boomer, hobbled him with a scrap of rope and let him graze. He poured dried beans in a pan of water to soak.

When the sun was low a coolness settled in. Arden built a little fire, chopped a strip of bacon into his pot and set it in the coals to boil. In the other pot he made coffee. Sprawled by the fire and the little stream, he felt a certain contentment he had not anticipated. He had no plans to stay in this forlorn country; he'd had enough, both of farming, and of roughing it in his younger years in the west. And yet the setting sun across the undulating prairie did have a certain beauty, and especially the native flowers. A coyote yipped and howled, answered by others far to his south. What other wildness did this land conceal? Likely a few wolves, maybe bobcats and a cougar or two. Nothing to fear, he was sure, other than maybe Indians. He dug out his revolver and checked that the cylinder was full.

Arden was hungry, and he pulled the bacon and beans from the fire. The beans required a lot of chewing; Maggie would have soaked them all day and they would be soft and much tastier than these. What was it she put in besides salt? Probably some chili pepper, something that gave them more kick. What was Maggie doing tonight, he wondered. Surely by now Bob Brady's body had been discovered, by stench if no other way. Did Maggie care about Bob, or was he just a convenient slob? What would she do now? Was she missing him? How would she support herself? At least she had the house. She was a pretty woman. She would make out somehow.

He had to stop thinking these thoughts, what he had done, what he'd left behind. There was no going back. If he did, and if the law didn't get him, the Brady boys would. He had to make a plan of some kind. He rolled a cigarette, touched it to the embers and lay back watching the flames dance. With all the free land here, and probably not enough settlers to fill it all, at least not right away, the piece he had grabbed wouldn't be worth much for awhile. He might as well hide out here as anyplace, but in the meantime he had to find a way to survive. He had enough provisions to last maybe two weeks, and there was surely game to kill, but in the long run he'd need a plan. He fed more brush onto the fire, rolled his blanket around him and reclined under a vast canopy of stars, the same open sky he remembered from nights on the Oregon Trail.

Repeatedly through the night he was awakened by a cacophony of coyote packs. Likely they had new pups to feed, and suddenly their territory had been invaded by hordes of people and horses. Their prey was likely in deep hiding, and both predator and prey were hungry and confused by the disruption of their world. A great horned owl was also hunting along Arden's creek, moving up and down the line, pausing to utter hoots that not only kept it in touch with its fellows and defined its territory, but also unnerved mice and birds and small creatures until finally one might flinch and dart from its cover, only to be nabbed by a fierce predator with the nighttime vision to spot movement from a hundred yards away.

When at last dawn broke in the eastern sky, Arden was well awake, if not rested. He threw off his blanket and shivered as he rekindled the fire and made coffee. He built up the fire and warmed himself while he fried bacon and potatoes. Soon the sun cleared the horizon and crept down the trees where he sheltered. He went to Boomer, who grazed calmly on the slope. Boomer whinnied softly as Arden approached, seemingly happy to be in a land of such bounty.

Arden unhobbled him, slipped the bridle around his head and led him to the creek for water. He threw on the blanket and saddle and tied Boomer to a tree. He found a place in tall thick grass to stash his possessions, mounted the stallion and rode back toward the river. He passed at a distance the farmer who'd taken his intended claim. The man was already at work with an ax, shaping small tree trunks for rafters to span a gully. When Arden reached the Cimarron he pointed Boomer southeast toward Kingfisher, where he'd been told he'd find the land office and could file his claim.

The office wasn't hard to find. When he arrived around noon, already a string of men stretched out the door and down the dusty street. He tied Boomer to a tree and joined the line. Most men were talkative and jovial, giddy at the prospect of filing a paper that would make them possessors of one hundred and sixty acres of land, something most of them had never experienced, and until recently never even imagined. He himself had never known such good fortune, a realization that was just beginning to sink in. He recalled the hilly sixty acre farm back in Missouri, where his father somehow thought a family could survive on rocky soil. Or maybe he simply never had another choice. Now Arden would have nearly three times the land—and better land.

At first he talked to nobody except in brief replies, but he listened to the excited chatter. People had brought all manner of seeds, wheat from Kansas, corn, garden seeds of every kind, even cotton some guy brought from Mississippi. Some had extra seed they wanted to sell or trade. Which of those crops would grow here, he wondered. But one thing was becoming ever more clear. Only he was without a plan. He had an excuse, of course. He'd left in a bit of a hurry. But he also didn't want to be a farmer. Maybe he could be a cop of some sort, if and when they had such things, but then it occurred to him that if he applied for such a position he would likely be asked for a reference, and that he couldn't give.

So what could he do to stay alive? He'd have to figure something, because he'd already spent half the meager savings he'd drawn from the bank. He had no real skills. Besides law enforcement, he'd worked as a mule skinner and a tie bedder on the railroad. There was no call for the former except on long distance trails, which now were being replaced by railroads, and the latter was hard work he didn't care to do again. He was good at poker, that he'd learned on long nights when nothing much was happening in Fort Scott. Maybe he could draw some of these hicks into a game.

Then he thought again about Boomer. Over the past two days he'd come to realize that he had bought a very fine horse. Boomer was strong and fast, tall and well shaped. Given the circumstances, he was probably worth considerably more than the twenty-five dollars Arden had paid. It came to his mind that he'd seen many a mare and gelding during the run, but stallions were in short supply. Surely he could put Boomer out to stud. Every farmer who'd come with one horse would need another for a team. There would be a good market for horses, and for other livestock. Boomer had gotten him where he needed to be to win a farm, but perhaps he could help support him now that they were here.

Arden struck up a conversation with the man in front of him, a man in overalls and worn out work shoes. "Say, know anybody with a good filly or mare? I happen to have a top dollar stud that would produce the best colts in the territory," he bragged.

"Is that right?" the man replied. "As a matter of fact, I made the run with a pair of mares, good wagon and plow horses, but they're not as strong as they used to be. What would you want for the service?"

"Well, normally with a horse of Boomer's quality I'd need ten dollars a head," Arden said, "but since we're all in this thing together, just to be a good neighbor I'd take five."

"Whew, five seems a little high to me," the man said. "I'd have to see your stud." Now they were at the front of the line. Arden stepped up, signed the paper he had filled out and plunked down twelve dollars, ten for the government and two for the land agent.

The other man's name was Jorsky. Turned out his claim was just a couple of miles past Arden's. Once they were through the line and had filed their papers, Arden took Jorsky out to see the stallion. Jorsky seemed satisfied. "So when one of your mares comes into heat just bring her over," Arden said. "I think Boomer here will be glad to be of service," he added with a laugh.

Arden led Boomer in front of the office. Every time a man came out he repeated his offer, and some seemed interested. He told people where to find him and said he was glad to be neighborly. By the end of the day he was offering a good deal on a date with a hundred dollar race horse for just five dollars a head.

As the sun sank low the last stragglers left the land office and headed back toward their claims. Arden suddenly felt so rich, at least in prospects, that he went back into the general store before it closed and bought a bag of tobacco, a bottle of whiskey and a slab of beef. It would be a long ride back to the claim, but the moon was nearly full. Tonight by his campfire he would celebrate.

CHAPTER 10

Reuben's eyes opened with a start. He must have dozed. It appeared to be mid morning, though the sky was so dark it was hard to tell. The rain still pounded his shoulders, but perhaps a little less intense. Ruth was asleep, at least he hoped she was. Her body sprawled across his legs and he squirmed to get comfortable. He took her wrist, and found a pulse. He wished for company, but he didn't want to wake her as long as she could somehow sleep.

Squinting through the rain Reuben made out the profile of two horses on the western bank, standing in the shelter of a cedar grove. He'd sold the last of his work horses long ago. It must have been about 1920, because it was soon after John came home from the World War and married Prairie Star. With John to help and with more land to farm, they'd bought a John Deere. Prairie Star had turned out to be a fine wife for John, though Reuben had certainly had his doubts at first. He had never really reconciled with her father, but in reality it was a two-way street. After all, he'd taken the quarter Arden Breedlove wanted, and he'd threatened to kill him to boot.

It was hard to see the horses go at the time, but how many times had he wished he'd sold them all, including the wild colt descended from Breedlove's stud? One more thing that he and Ruth rarely talked about. That was an impressive horse Breedlove had ridden that day, he had to admit, and alongside some shady dealings, Breedlove had built a good business, with the roan stallion as a start. But who would ever have guessed that Breedlove's daughter and his son would one day fall in love and marry? As a blacksmith Reuben had forged many a strong chain link, but the best of them was easy to break, he understood, compared to the chain of events called life. If he'd learned anything, it was that every decision, every action, is a link in a chain that you couldn't possibly foresee and untangle before it was too late to cut a particular link. Take the last horse, for example. If he could go back he would gladly put a bullet between the eyes of that filly the day she was born, just a week before John and Prairie Star's only child. The filly that as a mare would produce the colt that could never be trusted, but that Joseph insisted he could break and ride.

Reuben picked a spot on the bank and watched for what he judged to be a minute, trying to gauge how fast the flood was taking them, and how far they had come. The water was brown and swirling, but spread out across the plain as it was, the current was not swift. They floated above what seemed to be the channel, a wide strip marked by flotsam and foam. He guessed they might be moving a mile an hour. The water was moving considerably faster of course, but the vessel on which they rode was anything but sleek, half of its eight-foot height submerged. It bumped now and then against unseen junk or brush or a floating log, bobbing and turning aimlessly like other scraps of debris. A steel cattle tank was passing them, half full of rain but still riding high. If only the tank would come closer. Reuben's throat ached with thirst, but there was no clean water to be had. Now far back from the bank stood another collection of small buildings, a few trees and what looked like a Hereford cow.

Reuben thought about Rosie. When he opened the barn door, did she plunge madly into the current and float away, or did she manage to scramble toward land? She was a good milk cow, Rosie. She gave enough every day for all their needs, the surplus going to John and Prairie Star and even the scruffy cats that lived in the barn. If only they'd had her that first year, things might have been different. It was the greatest gulf that lay between Ruth and him, the other thing they didn't talk about. Sometimes sitting by the fire in their snug modern home they would reminisce about the early days, about their first crude shelters, about the other struggles they had endured. But without ever having agreed to let the one subject lie, they did not talk about Jacob. Ruth might mention the damp cold of the dugout, the centipedes on the wall, field mice in the flour, the bull snake that came for the mice, long dark winter days. She might talk about the luxury of a bath tub and toilet for people who had gone without bathing for many days, and for the young wife who had no choice but to eliminate her waste in a stinking porcelain pot with a complete lack of privacy. She would sometimes even recall hungry nights and days. But never did she mention the horrifying ordeal of watching her firstborn waste away. Perhaps over time the wound would have healed if only they could have talked. They had finally been able to talk about Joseph, but by that time years of disappointments and living near the edge had thickened the hides of their hearts, and to some degree hardened them to grief, had taught them that life is a process of giving up.

That first loss was never far from Reuben's mind either, but he always knew when the dark cloud had descended on Ruth. With the money he'd spent on the gun he might have bought the cow. Of course that likely would have meant losing a second claim, something he vowed not to do. But there were other quarters farther west he could have taken, perhaps some just as good. Then it occurred to him that if he had foregone the gun and walked patiently west that day until he found a good quarter nobody else desired, he and Ruth would not be floating down the Cimarron today, facing the possibility that it would be their watery grave. If there was anything living eighty-nine years told you, it was that every choice you make will have consequences down the line that you could not, and perhaps would not foresee, that every day brings forks in the road, and those who would truly live must choose. He had chosen, not just that day, but many crucial days since, and those choices were his life.

Now Ruth stirred and jerked stiff across Reuben's knees. She opened her eyes and stared blindly ahead across Reuben's soaked pants legs, the shingled roof, the churning waters, the distant hills. At last she spoke. "I was dreaming," she said, "dreaming of the first time I crossed the Cimarron. It was in Papa's wagon, everything we owned piled high. You pointed out the dugout at the edge of the bluff. The river was low, so we thought we could make it. Then came a flood and everything was washed away." Her voice trailed off and the only sound was raindrops on their raincoats and on the mossy roof.

"Well," Reuben said when he'd summoned the meager reserve of energy he felt, "we did make it that day, and we'll make it again."

"No," Ruth said. "We won't make it again. I saw in my dream how it will end."

"Don't talk like that Ruth," he said. "Sooner or later the current will take us to shore and we'll be saved. Look, hasn't the rain eased up a little? We've been through a lot since the first time we crossed, and we'll weather this too."

Her first time to cross was of course not his. He had crossed in the night to choose a place. He had crossed again and climbed the bluff the next noon to stake his claim. Once he'd established a first rude structure he had crossed yet again, walked back to Hennessey and hopped another freight back to Wichita to get Ruth so that they could cross together to the golden life that awaited them.

But on his second day Reuben had taken his axe and rope back down the bluff to the river. He cut a dozen young willow trees and tied them together. While he was at work, two young Indian men approached him. One spoke a few words of English, demanding that he stop, claiming that if settlers cut down the trees the deer and turkeys they hunted to feed their children would leave. He waited until they were far down the river and resumed his work. It took all afternoon to drag the trees up the bluff. His ankle still pained him, but it was something he had to ignore. Exerting all his youthful power he could drag the dozen small trunks lashed together with a scrap of rope just a few feet at a time before he had to catch his breath. As the sun set he reached the top and lugged them across prairie grasses to the little ravine at the edge.

Before dawn Reuben woke to the blood curdling howl of a wolf, somewhere just outside his tarp. He fumbled for the Colt and flung the canvas aside. He saw nothing in the darkness but a faint glow across the Cimarron. He was well awake now, so he crawled outside, chewed a biscuit and a string of jerky and gathered his tools. Now the eastern sky was brighter, and he was alarmed to see in the earth he had disturbed the distinct print of a huge canine paw. He was glad he had kept his meager ration of food inside, and that by tonight he would have a more substantial shelter prepared.

With his axe he whittled away at the earthen edges, shaping a room eight feet wide and sixteen long. Two upright willow trunks framed an opening overlooking the Cimarron. The other ten spanned the cut. He arranged the limbs and twigs perpendicular to the rafters, then covered the roof with the canvas he'd brought. The edges were secured with stones from the marker pile. The skull he hid away in a clump of wild plums. No need for Ruth to be haunted by that.

Now that he had a shelter, Reuben used his axe to till a small plot near the spring. Too bad he couldn't have brought the shovel, but more basic tools like the axe, the tarp and the rope had been heavy and bulky enough. He was amazed that he'd made it to the top so fast that day with what must have been thirty pounds on his back. He chopped a small plot of prairie until it was loose, cut most of the potatoes he'd brought into small pieces, each piece with an eye, and planted them in soil that had never been turned. He hoped that by the time Ruth was here they would be sprouted. He built a little fire, wolfed down some jerky and biscuits and rolled out his blanket in their new home.

Across the Cimarron

On the fourth day Reuben threw off his blanket at first light, stashed everything he'd brought in the brush where he'd hidden the skull, except a little food, a canteen of water and the Colt. He was tortured by the fact that he hadn't filed the claim, and it was still possible somebody else would cheat him out of his land. But that meant a long trip to Kingfisher, which on foot might take two days to go and return. He'd been gone nearly a week and he knew Ruth would be worried, so he'd decided to risk waiting to file until he could return with her. He picked his way down the steep incline to the river's edge. Again he plunged into the cold water, waded and swam, emerged shivering on the eastern bank and strode toward Hennessey. His ankle was much better now, and he covered the fifteen miles before noon. The train wasn't expected until two, so he moved up the tracks and stretched out in a clump of trees to wait.

He awoke to the whistle. The train seemed to consist mostly of cattle cars, all of them full, and it wasn't going to stop. When it slowed he ran beside it and swung himself up the ladder and onto the ledge above the hitch. The irregularities of the tracks were jarring to his hips if he sat, so he stood, absorbing the shock in his knees, and watched the world of 1889 go by, the two and a half miles of homesteads that stretched to the line between Unassigned Lands and the Cherokee Strip. Then it was undeveloped prairie once more, low rolling hills of grass and wooded streams that would run to the Kansas line.

When the train slowed to stop at Caldwell for water and fuel he climbed on top and hid himself by lying flat, then climbed back down and stood again when they picked up speed. Steers bumped and bawled, and the wind whipped their urine his way. It was a long ride, hopefully the next to last ride he would pinch from the railroad. Someday he and Ruth would ride back to visit her parents on the passenger train. When they pulled into the Wichita stockyards at dusk he jumped off and walked toward Ruth's parents' home.

How long she had watched for him, he had no idea. For most of a week she'd had no way to know if he was alive or dead, whether he had succeeded this time, or failed again. But there she was at the window gazing out, her profile outlined by light of the kerosene lamp. He rushed across the yard and knocked on the door. In seconds she was in his arms, he lifting her off her feet and swinging her around and around. "We have a farm!" he exclaimed. "We have a farm!"

And then her father and mother were there, all locked in an embrace of celebration and joy. "I knew you would get a place this time," James said. "You're not the kind of son-in-law who is going to let somebody steal your place a second time." Abigail ushered them into the kitchen, where she sat Reuben down at the table. She brought out the leftovers from supper and put the pot on the stove to heat, a thick stew of vegetables and beef. For the first time in a week Reuben ate a rich hot meal while they showered him with questions. He shoveled down the food and described the place.

"The soil might not be as good as the river bottom I should have had in eighty-nine," he said. "It's on a high bluff above the Cimarron, and the soil is red and hard, but last year's grasses reach above my waist, so I think it will grow good wheat. There's a sweet water spring and a little creek, and yes," he added to Ruth, "we'll have a garden watered from the spring. We should be able to grow everything we need."

They asked him to tell about the run, whether he encountered any claim jumpers, how he was able to compete on foot with those on horseback. He told about the plunge across the icy river, the struggle up the crumbling bluff, the sprint to the marker. "It was really pretty easy," he said. He didn't mention the man on the roan stallion, the gun, or the skull that peered out from the pile of rocks.

And then they were off to bed. Never had Ruth's slender young body felt so good, and never had they loved so hard and well. Even if he had returned empty-handed, the homecoming would have been worth the long days of struggle. But he was not empty-handed. They had a claim. Tomorrow they would load their possessions on Ruth's father's wagon, and the next day set out to their new life west of the Cimarron.

There wasn't that much to load. The only heavy item was the porcelain-faced cook stove, the oven of which contained family treasures and Reuben's fiddle, bundled amongst blankets. James and Reuben lugged the heavy cast iron piece out of the back room and onto the wagon. Around the stove they packed a bed, a crude table and two chairs, the chest that held their clothing, a rug, a little lumber Reuben had salvaged from a carpenter job, his tools for carpentry, gardening and blacksmithing, a grinder for coffee and wheat, vegetable seeds and the seed wheat he had saved, jars of fruit and vegetables Ruth and Abigail had canned, Abigail's older pots and pans and the extra jars she could spare, kitchen goods, a family photograph, the salt, sugar, coffee, flour and oil Ruth had bought from their meager savings, and other items necessary for a new life on the claim. They dug up ten volunteer apple, peach, pear and cherry trees and packed them in wet burlap.

Ruth's parents begged them to stay another day and rest, but Reuben still had not filed the claim and he feared that somebody else would file in his stead. So very early next morning they had a big breakfast, packed food into a wooden box and filled a five gallon crock with water. While Reuben harnessed James' team, an aging mare and a mule, James went to the chicken house and caught half a dozen hens from their flock. He deposited them in a coop he had made, then strapped the chickens and their cage on the back of the wagon. Reuben clucked the team into action, they waved and called goodbye, and by dawn they were headed south on the Chisholm Trail. They had a hundred and fifty miles to go, and it was anybody's guess how far this mismatched team could haul them and their possessions in a day.

The first day they covered at least forty miles, camping on the Chikaskia River north of Caldwell. The team was not accustomed to this kind of workout, and even though Reuben had rested them several times along the way, they were beat. He built a fire, then unhitched the team and hobbled them to graze and drink at the river's edge while Ruth cooked supper.

The second night they camped on Red Rock Creek, the third on the bluff west of Hennessey. A fellow camper showed them a wooden marker where in 1874 freighter Pat Hennessey and three other men hauling sugar and coffee had been murdered, lashed to a wagon wheel and burned. On the fourth day Reuben harnessed the team very early and they headed west toward the Cimarron. The mare shied when he tried to drive them into the river. He grasped a bridle in each hand and led them in. He pulled until the water reached his armpits, then swam with the reins in one hand. Once they were in the middle of the river the mare and the mule ceased their protest and plunged eagerly toward the western bank.

Reuben headed them south along the trail, now well-worn by thousands of hooves and hundreds of wagons, south the way he had crept that first night to the mouth of the salty creek and up its valley to the mouth of Spring Creek. There the trail was steep, and in spite of his coaxing and even lashing their hind quarters with a branch, the team could not pull the loaded wagon up the hill.

The sun was sinking low, but there was only one thing to do. Reuben and Ruth unloaded everything except the stove. Now the team was rested, and finally they managed to drag the lighter wagon up the hill. Then Ruth and Reuben carried all the things they had left behind up the incline, repacked the wagon and rolled by light of the first twinkling stars across the last half mile to the dugout Reuben had carved in the edge of the bluff. Again they unloaded all but the stove and carried everything to the little cave. They spread the rug on the dirt floor, piled their possessions along one wall and set up the bed. Now the moon was rising in the east, casting its light into the little hovel, on the bed and on Reuben and Ruth as they embraced, took off their clothes and snuggled under the quilt Ruth's mother had made.

CHAPTER 12

In the morning they dragged the heavy stove off the wagon and set it up beside the dugout. It would have filled a quarter of the space in their shelter, and with summer coming it made more sense to cook outside for now. Reuben unpacked his tools, sawed rough planks, nailed them together and attached them to the doorpost with leather straps. Now that they had a door their house was complete. Unfortunately they had no glass, so with the door closed the only light was splinters of sunlight or moonlight that filtered through the cracks. But soon summer would be here and the door could remain open most of the time. On the inside he attached a hasp so the door could be secured.

And now the trip must be made again. He thought of taking Ruth with him, but they didn't have the money for train tickets, and though she could have walked back from Hennessey, he was pretty sure she couldn't safely jump off a moving freight train. She would have to stay alone while he returned the wagon and team. Anyway, he could travel faster with the wagon empty, hopefully make it to Wichita in three days and back on the fourth.

His father-in-law's team was exhausted by the four day journey, so he would let them rest a couple of days. He hobbled them by the creek where there was plenty of water and the grass was lush. While Ruth unpacked kitchen utensils, Reuben chopped down a few more willows and built a small, moveable enclosure for the hens. There were already plenty of insects and earthworms to be had, and the cage could be moved to a new grassy spot each day. Then he and Ruth transplanted the apple, cherry, peach and pear saplings on a slope near the spring, to where water could be carried when needed. He spaded a garden plot beside the potatoes, and they planted the first of the seeds they had brought—lettuce, spinach, turnips, onions, and peas.

Reuben didn't worry about the coyotes or wolves he knew were there, or even the bobcats and cougars that likely roamed the river country. The cage would keep the hens safe, and the door would keep animals out of the dugout. But he did worry about Indians. The bison were virtually exterminated by now, and even the bones left after the slaughter had been picked up by scavengers over the past decade or two and hauled away to make fertilizer. But he'd heard at Hennessey about the Ghost Dances in the Indian camp at Cantonment, a ritual brought from Nevada to Indian Territory a couple of years earlier by a Paiute named Wovoka. Wovoka had whipped Indians across the Great Plains into a frenzy with his prophecy of the extinction of white people and the return of the buffalo and traditional ways of life. Reuben had heard rumors that unhappy Cheyennes and Arapahos were lurking along the river, apparently refusing to move to the quarter sections they'd been allotted, and that one chief had even warned settlers to leave "within three sleeps." He hadn't seen Indians since his second day by the river, and three sleeps had long since passed, but he had seen what appeared to be moccasin tracks at the spring. He had not shared his apprehension with Ruth, but after supper he brought out the revolver, which he had wrapped in cloth and stashed in the bottom of his tool chest.

At first she recoiled at the sight, but her repulsion was soon replaced by questions about where he had obtained the gun and how much it had cost. She reminded him of other things they badly needed, things eight dollars would have bought, and for the first time in their marriage she questioned his judgment. He justified the purchase by reminding her what happened in 1889, but wondered if he had only increased her fears of staying alone. He didn't tell her about potentially hostile Indians or the scar-faced man he had threatened to kill. Instead he talked about the unlikely threat from wild animals, and eventually coaxed her to hold the weapon in her hands. He put two of his scarce cartridges in the cylinder and showed her how to sight and shoot. The first shot jerked the gun into the air. The second she held steady.

They were up early next morning, and the mare and the mule were splashing across the river at dawn. Ruth watched from the bluff as the wagon rolled slowly east, finally disappearing behind a sand dune. She reasoned that Reuben knew more than he had told her; she too had read in the Wichita paper about the Ghost Dancers and the unrest over the loss of land. She picked up the revolver, heavy and cold in her hands. She brought it up and sighted on a blackjack trunk on the cliff. She felt the trigger. She was pretty sure she could fire the gun again, but firing at another human, or even an animal, was something she had never contemplated. She laid it on the kitchen table and went out to drag the chicken coup to fresh grass.

Ruth realized with a shudder that she was completely alone. Had she ever experienced this before? She searched memory for a time when there was no human nearby, or at least within earshot, and came up empty. She sat down on the marker rocks and surveyed the river valley that stretched from northwest to southeast as far as her eye could see. She too had seen the tracks of coyote's and wolves, and now something moved in the brush at the river's edge. She squinted her eyes and watched until it moved again. It was a deer, browsing on willow shoots by the water. Meadowlarks and other birds she did not know were singing, but the only other sound was a gentle wind that ruffled the fresh cottonwood leaves at the spring. She turned her gaze to survey their claim, her claim too, she realized. She had never owned land before, nor had her parents, nor anybody else she knew. The idea took some getting used to, the idea of owning. Were they rich, or would they be? She felt confident that she and Reuben would survive on this land, but it wasn't exactly clear just how. But wasn't it beautiful! Prairie flowers were blooming, the rising sun warm. She got up and walked to the spring.

The water was cold, just emerging from the earth. She realized that she had not bathed for days. She looked around at the solitude, unbuttoned and dropped her dress on the grass and stepped into the water. She squatted and splashed the cold elixir over her body, then emerged shivering and stretched out on the grass to dry in the sun.

"Enough of this laziness," she mumbled at last. "There is work to do." She pulled on her clothing and shoes and went back to the dugout for a hoe and seeds. Reuben had spaded a plot a hundred feet long, and there was more planting to do, corn, beans, pumpkins and squash. When she finished that, she also needed to gather more cow pies for the stove. The government had officially expelled the cattlemen from Cheyenne Arapaho land in 1885, so most of the dung was badly deteriorated and had little fuel value. But she could also gather sticks along the waterway, and for now she needed only enough for cooking. For winter they would need real fuel, wood cut by the river or elsewhere and somehow hauled up the hill to their home.

What made her look back over her shoulder toward their dwelling, she didn't know. But when she did, two men, long black braids and naked above the waist, were just disappearing inside the dugout! What could she do? She had left the gun inside. Now they would find it and could kill her, and nobody would ever know what happened. She thought of rushing to the house, but her feet were frozen. Instead she crouched amongst the trees and watched.

After what seemed a long time, the pair emerged. They had nothing in their hands; they had left the revolver. They stared out across the Cimarron for awhile, conversed briefly in words she could barely hear and did not understand, then walked straight toward her!

When they saw her crouching amongst the leaves they stopped, looked at each other, and spoke more words. One gestured toward her, then they resumed their stroll in her direction. When they were close one raised his voice and called something to her. She had no response, and he repeated his words. They came closer still, and finally they were close enough to touch. She stood. "Hello," she stammered. "My name is Ruth." Then she extended her hand. The pair looked at each other, then the older one touched her hand lightly and made a little nod. They resumed their talk, words that had no meaning for her.

The men dropped to their knees, cupped their hands and drank. The older one spoke again, and they stepped across the creek. She watched them walk west and eventually disappear over the rise. Only then did she realize that her heart had been pounding. She breathed deeply and headed for the dugout. Nothing had been disturbed. It appeared they meant her no harm.

The second day Ruth awoke feeling ill. She opened the door and went outside, feeling that she might throw up. "Just nerves," she mumbled. "But I have to be strong." She tidied up the house, that is she organized the kitchen utensils and food in a small cabinet and brushed the dust and debris that had fallen from the roof off the table and bed. With the morning light shining in, she could see how primitive their accommodations were, close to barbaric. Her parents had never had any extra money, but she had grown up in a snug, clean framed house. She hoped they would not be in this cave for long.

Each day she moved the chicken crate and gathered the eggs, usually four or five, one day six. She ate one for breakfast each morning, but horded the rest in the cabinet, a kind of wealth in a place where otherwise life was on the margins. On the fourth morning she felt sick to her stomach again. She didn't even feel like eating breakfast. Instead she sat on the rocks and watched for Reuben, but he did not come. She knew it was unrealistic to expect him this soon, but he had said possibly four days, so her eyes were drawn to the trail that emerged from the sandy hills. Throughout the day she found herself feeling nervous and fearful. Perhaps it was just loneliness; certainly she had never before been alone for four days. She knew there had to be other settlers in the neighborhood, but she had no idea where. She once thought of exploring along the bluff to see if she might find a friendly neighbor, but what if instead she found ruffians or hostile Indians? She couldn't make herself leave the small area defined by the spring and its little creek, the orchard, the garden and the dugout. She wished for some work to do, but the garden and orchard were just planted and needed no hoeing. She had gathered a substantial pile of cooking fuel. She took the bucket to the spring and carried water to the fruit trees, even though the soil was still damp from the day before.

As the sun was setting she positioned herself on the rock pile to wait. The moon was in its last quarter now, so it would not be up soon. Finally it was too dark to make out the river or the sand hills, let alone a man who might be trudging up the trail. She retreated to the shelter and closed the door. But she could not sleep. Reuben should be here by now, she told herself. Something had gone wrong.

At last she did fall into a deep sleep, and in her dreams she heard the voices of the men who had found her at the spring. They were outside the door, demanding to be let in. Then the door shook. She groped on the table for the gun and pointed it at the door. Then there was Reuben's voice, "Beautiful woman," he called, "could you let a weary traveler in?"

She sprang from the bed, replaced the revolver on the table and opened the door. Then she was in his arms, shedding tears of relief and joy. "I've been so lonely without you," she murmured.

"Not half as lonely as me," he replied.

Now the half moon had risen. He took her by the hand and they walked to the spring. He took off his dusty clothes and plunged into the creek, splashing and washing away the dirt of the road. Then she was with him, naked in the moonlight, their feet in the icy spring, their hearts joined in happiness and love.

CHAPTER 13

More than two weeks had now passed since the run. Reuben had walked to Kingfisher and filed his claim. The potatoes he had planted the third day were peeking through the soil, and here and there a tiny seedling of lettuce, spinach, turnip, onion and pea. The corn, beans, pumpkins and squash would be up soon. A thunderstorm had passed in the night, and their roof barely leaked, just one spot where a crease in the canvas formed a pond. Ruth threw open the door. The morning was fresh and bright.

"What do you say we take a holiday, my dear," Reuben proposed. "Go see if we can find any new neighbors at home."

"That would be great," Ruth replied. But she didn't feel so great. Again a nagging nausea gripped her stomach. Reuben noticed her hands on her abdomen and the pained expression on her face.

"Is something wrong?" he asked.

"Just that I haven't felt so well the last couple of mornings. Probably too much sameness in our diet. I'm sure I'll be OK." But she did begin to wonder. She tried to remember back to her last period. She couldn't put her finger on it, but it seemed like well over a month ago. Was she pregnant? The thought both thrilled and frightened her. She certainly wanted to have a child with Reuben, but under these conditions? She decided not to mention these thoughts just yet, to wait and see, but she did tell Reuben about the two visitors she had had while he was gone. He was alarmed, but she assured him that the Indians seemed to mean no harm.

Reuben built a fire in the stove, and Ruth fried fresh bacon he had brought, along with eggs from their hens. Then hand in hand they set out across the bluff to discover who else was inhabiting the land. When they came to the ravine, a wagon load of lumber was starting up the hill, pulled by a pair of black work horses. The pair sat under a cottonwood on a fallen log to wait, feet dangling in the air.

"Hello!" Reuben called when the man was within earshot. The man waved back. Now he was off the wagon, leading the team and urging them on. He was a barrel-chested man of thirty or so, dressed in dungarees and a leather vest. He paused at the top and offered his hand. "I'm Peter Weber," he said in a heavy German accent.

Reuben introduced himself and Ruth and asked if they could give a hand. "Of course," Weber said. "My place is just over the ridge. As you can see, I have materials to build a small house." The three walked together before the team. They crossed the ridge and entered a small green valley with a long view across the river. In the middle was a pile of possessions covered by a tarp, one edge held down by a plow, the other by a bucket of water. Weber brought the team to a halt. "Here's the spot," he said, gesturing in a small circle to indicate the perimeters of the house and yard he saw in his mind.

Reuben and Peter untied the lumber and began to unload the unhewn boards, four by four beams for a plate, two by sixes for joists, two by fours for studs and rafters and rough planks for walls and roof. A roll of heavy tar paper would keep out the wind and rain until the walls and roof could be sided and shingled. There was even a manufactured window and door. "It will be small at first," Peter said apologetically, "just twelve by sixteen, but I can add on."

"That sounds wonderful," Ruth said, thinking of the dark hovel in which they lived. "And is there a Mrs. Weber?" she added hopefully.

"There is," Peter said. "Her name is Esther. I'll go for her once the house is built. She's been a little sick of late, and we thought it best that she stay in Caldwell until the house is ready."

"I've done a fair amount of carpenter work," Reuben ventured, "in case you might need a hand with the heavy work."

84

"That would be wonderful," the new neighbor said. "I've spent most of our savings on the lumber, and I couldn't pay you much, but maybe we could work out a trade." Reuben had been eyeing the strong work horses, still sweating from the pull up the bluff and flicking flies with their tails.

"Well, I don't know how your horses would feel about this, but how about I help you build your house and you loan your horses and plow so I can strip off some sod for a house and plow a patch of prairie to plant wheat this fall?"

"I like that idea," Weber said with a laugh. "You and my horses trade work and I get off pretty easy."

Weber brought out a loaf of bread he'd bought in Hennessey and some cheese and even a bottle of wine. He produced three glasses and they sat on the grass and ate. "Here's to neighbors and the neighborhood!" Weber boomed, raising his glass.

Early next morning Reuben walked to Weber's place with his hammer and saw and other tools, and for the next couple of weeks he crossed the ridge each day. The little house rose quickly, a tight house with a small stove in the corner, space for a kitchen cabinet, a table and four chairs, a wardrobe and bed, even a small love seat that Peter's mother had brought from Germany. At noon Ruth crossed the ridge with a basket of food, sometimes fresh bread she'd baked on the outside stove, boiled eggs from their hens, even tender leaves of lettuce and spinach.

When the door was hung, both men set to the task of plowing prairie sod. It was a laborious process, turning native prairie that had never been disturbed, dense earth bound together by a tangle of roots. Weber's horses pulled with all their might, and the one bottom plow sheered the roots and turned the soil. Since his neighbor had no seed wheat, Reuben offered, with some trepidation, to trade half his seed for other future use of the wagon and team. He would plant just ten acres in September rather than the twenty he had planned. He realized that working down even ten acres to a good seed bed would be hard enough, since he had other pressing concerns, such as building a sod house to replace the dugout.

Ruth hadn't complained about the dust in the food and on the bed or the insects on their walls, but they both looked with envy on their new neighbor's snug frame home. If only they could somehow have accumulated a hundred dollars, they too could have a wagon and team and buy some lumber to start a real house. But their savings now totaled more like ten dollars, and before they could harvest and sell a crop of wheat the next summer there were pressing necessities, such as staple foods. They had brought canned fruits and vegetables from Kansas, and for the summer they should be able to survive with produce from their garden, perhaps supplemented with a little wild game—what could be snared or shot with a pistol—but winter would come all too soon, and Reuben worried they would not be prepared.

He would plant winter wheat in early fall, but he didn't know what kind of yield to expect. Fields he had worked in Kansas made more than twenty bushels per acre in good years. His wheat would grow in virgin soil, so it might do better. But the price of wheat had fallen steadily for a couple of decades, from well over a dollar a bushel when he was a boy to seventy cents, and as production increased across the plains, talk was that it would fall even lower. If the price held steady and he raised twenty bushels per acre, that would be two hundred bushels. After saving some for Ruth's bread making and for replanting an enlarged field, he might be able to sell one hundred fifty bushels, which might bring a hundred dollars, though he had no idea how much of that the railroad would charge for shipping.

Reuben made these calculations over and over, sometimes even in his dreams. If the weather was good and the market held, by the next summer they might have enough to buy a wagon, a team and at least enough lumber to roof a sod house. There was no way a framed house could be squeezed from such calculations; that would have to wait. If he had a good crop and no market, what would be the point? If there was a good market and no crop, the same. As spring turned to summer there was little rain, so optimism came hard.

From an edge of the ten acres he had marked Reuben held the plow steady so it would peel off the sod six inches deep. With Weber's wagon he hauled the earth to a flat place on the bluff beside the dugout, marked out the dimensions, and began to lay out layers of sod, overlapping each for strength. There would be one room, fourteen by twenty feet, a door in the east, small openings on north and south that could be shuttered in winter and opened when weather was warm. The walls were twelve inches thick, the width of the sod-breaking plow. He stacked the sod seven feet high. The floor would be mere earth, carpeted with prairie grass.

If only he had the money to buy rafters and sheet iron or shingles for a roof. But the money wasn't there. Brush and the tarp would have to suffice for a roof the first winter, but at least they would have a house rather than a hovel, and before cold weather they would move the stove inside and lay in a supply of firewood.

While Peter finished details on his house, Reuben borrowed the team and wagon again, and he and Ruth drove west toward what he'd heard called the Gloss Mountains, twenty miles away. A ragged trail was already defining itself over the ridge and west to the new little town of Okeene, a collection of tents and a pair of quickly thrown up buildings that called themselves a hotel and saloon and a general store. The name of the place, they learned, was cobbled together from the words Oklahoma, Cherokee and Cheyenne. At Okeene they were half way, and the trail disappeared. But a low ragged mesa loomed on the western horizon, a long flat-topped skyline to shoot for.

Neither Ruth nor Reuben had ever seen a sight quite like the Gloss Mountains. To use the term "mountain" seemed an exaggeration; they were actually low buttes—rugged, dry clay and gypsum hills laced with selenite that reflected light like shiny glass. The valleys were rich with red cedars and other trees and with signs of wildlife, the buttes covered with cactus and sage.

By early afternoon Reuben had chopped down and stripped enough slender cedar trees for a ridgepole and rafters. They rested and had lunch in the shade of a cottonwood. Strange birds darted across the clearing, what they would later come to know as road runners. They loaded the slender logs, chopped dead limbs for firewood, piled the branches on top and turned the team back east.

In front of them something moved. A pair of huge diamond-backed rattlesnakes were warming themselves in the sun. Reuben steered the team away, but as they passed by the big snakes coiled, ready to strike. He had brought the Colt of course, but there was no need to waste ammunition. But having it was good, because the next thing they spotted was a fat tom turkey strutting with tail fanned. Besides the load of logs and cedar branches, they brought home a wild turkey to eat, the first fresh meat they'd have.

They reached Okeene at dusk, and followed the faint trail home by starlight. They arrived at the homestead well after dark, pulled the wagon beside a sod wall, unhitched and watered the team and crawled into bed. Next morning would be soon enough to unload and return the wagon so Peter could set out for Caldwell to get his furniture and his wife. Ruth would bake the turkey and can the leftover meat. She would prepare a welcoming feast when the Webers returned.

Chapter 14

When morning came, Reuben encircled his wife in his arms and pulled her close. "Good morning sweetheart," he whispered in her ear. Ruth opened her eyes to the dirt wall of the dugout, dimly lighted by splinters of sun that penetrated cracks around the door. She muttered a reply, and snuggled close.

The embrace was brief. Reuben threw off the covers and stepped into his pants. There was much to be done. Ruth knew that too. She needed to be up, making coffee and breakfast, helping unload the wagon, helping Reuben lug the cedar beams above the sod walls. There was water to be fetched, clothes to wash in the tub, an emerging garden to hoe. The most pressing task, she now recalled, was plucking and dismembering a turkey to cook. But the thought of gutting and cutting up a turkey made her stomach turn. She pulled herself up and reached for her dress.

When she bent over for her shoes her churning stomach made her swoon. She caught herself, sat on the bed and pulled on her shoes. Reuben was already out the door and the morning sun was streaming in. Suddenly Ruth lunged toward the opening, and just cleared the house when a wave of nausea doubled her. She dropped to hands and knees and wretched. Reuben heard the heave and rushed to her. "What is it Ruth?" he asked, now on his knees at her side. "Are you all right?"

She wiped her mouth with the back of her hand and struggled to stand. "I don't know," she answered. "I felt this way a couple of mornings while you were gone, but never this bad. Maybe it's something I ate.... Or," she said after a bit, now leaning on Reuben's shoulder, "it could be that I'm going to have a baby." She looked at him with tired wistful eyes, longing and fearful at the same time.

"Why, that would be wonderful!" Reuben boomed. "That's exactly what I've been hoping for. Look how everything is falling into place for us, darling, finding each other, getting this beautiful place at last, and now a child! We're living a dream!"

Ruth wasn't so sure. She too had looked forward to being pregnant, to bringing them a child. She couldn't ask for a better husband, and yes, she shared his hope and enthusiasm for this place. But she wasn't at all sure that this was the time. They were still living in the earth like rodents, and even the sod house would be tiny and raw, and probably cold and dark when winter came. Right now she felt more like crawling back into bed and covering her head than in facing a day in which new expectations were clouded by fear.

Reuben brought her a chair in the sun and a pan of water. She splashed her face and rinsed the bitterness from her mouth, then took a long drink from the dipper he offered. She remembered her mother's advice for when this time came. She pulled a bit of bread off a loaf, chewed it slowly and swallowed it with another drink of water. Reuben stood behind her, massaging her shoulders and muttering comfort.

Now she was feeling better. She tried to remember when her last period had come. She recalled it was in the first quarter of the moon, and now the moon was gone. It must have been at least six weeks. She must have already been pregnant when Reuben left that morning in April to seek this claim. "Yes," she said at last, mustering all the cheer she could, "I think I might be carrying a baby."

Reuben knelt and embraced her again, kissing her sweet and long. Then he abruptly rose. "Well, then I'd best get a better house built," he said. "We can't expect a new mother and baby to live out the winter in a cave!" He was on the wagon, throwing off brush, then standing the logs against the sod wall, working even faster than his usual driven pace.

Just as the wagon was empty and the horses were harnessed, Peter Weber appeared over the rise. They shared bread, potatoes, eggs and coffee, then Peter helped Reuben stand two end posts inside the walls and lash a center beam from end to end. After he was gone Reuben could single-handedly hoist the rafters up and

Ruth could hold them from the far side with a rope while he drove in spikes. By sundown the rafters were in place. Tomorrow he would cover the roof with leafy branches and lash the tarpaulin over the roof, and they would be ready to move in.

CHAPTER 15

Reuben eyed the sodden, weather-worn shingles of the chicken house roof to which they clung. The shingles were old, maybe forty years old, but they were cedar, and they had never leaked. If only they'd had money for lumber and shingles or sheet iron for a proper roof that first winter instead of brush covered with a rotting tarp, things might have gone differently. The canvas had still seemed strong when he stretched it across the roof in June, but blazing sun quickly deteriorated the fabric, and the fierce winds of thunderstorms whipped the cover so violently that soon small rips appeared. Reuben climbed the ladder he'd built from cedar poles and stitched the gashes together, but by summer's end the tarp was tattered. He sealed the stitches as best he could with tar, but he worried about whether the roof would keep out winter rains and wind.

All summer long the chickens laid, even more than Ruth and Reuben could use. When Peter Weber returned with his wife Esther, he also brought a hundred pound sack of flour and a big can of oil, as well as lots of sugar and coffee. Reuben and Ruth traded extra eggs and garden vegetables to the Webers for a share of these things they couldn't grow. They had plenty to eat from the garden—beans and peas, corn and potatoes and squash, spinach and other greens and soon there would be more tomatoes than they could possibly use. As Ruth's belly began to swell, she worked tirelessly, her pressure cooker simmering on the stove with jar after jar of vegetables for winter. After they moved into the sod house, the abandoned dugout made a perfect cellar for storing preserved vegetables and excess potatoes.

The summer was confirming Reuben's fears, proving drier than he had been led to expect from stories he'd heard about this

Eden west of the Cimarron. He carried bucket after bucket of water from the spring and kept the garden thriving. Though he couldn't stop worrying about the roof, at least it appeared they would have enough food to survive the winter. But with Ruth pregnant she needed milk, and neither they nor the Webers had a cow.

Every quarter section in the area had been claimed, so there were other neighbors, of course. Several were single men, some who seemed to have little idea what surviving on this raw plain might require, others who quickly disappeared once their claim was filed. Instead of planting a garden, one settler built a still, assuming the way to survive was to trade moonshine whiskey for supplies in town. But other than the Webers, Ruth and Reuben had encountered only one family close by, Rupert and Molly Dugan, who'd homesteaded with two small children a mile west. The Dugans had come from the hills of east Tennessee, moving slowly westward over a period of years, working as share-croppers or at whatever labor Rupert might find. Like the Westerfields, the Dugans had no money, but they did have a Jersey cow.

This Reuben learned when the cow strayed and Reuben found her enjoying the spinach patch. He yelled at the beast and drove her out, then threw a rope around her neck and followed her trail through the grass, over the hill to the Dugan homestead. It was a pitiful abode, to be sure, offering less comfort and protection than the Westerfields' now abandoned dugout. It was a small shallow hole with the removed dirt piled along the edges, brush and scraps of canvas as a roof. Two paint ponies tied to stakes and a shabbily covered wagon were the only visible possessions. When Reuben appeared with the cow in tow, the four Dugans emerged to greet him, a boy and a girl hiding behind their mother's torn and grimy dress. After three months, the Dugans seemed still to be living mostly in the wagon.

Reuben introduced himself and they thanked him for returning their cow. As they talked he looked around, but saw no sign of a garden or other preparations for winter. Eventually he ventured to ask about their plans. "Oh, we'll be heading back to civilization," Rupert Dugan said. "No human being could spend the winter out here in the wilds without a proper house. The wife's people have an extra room over at Guthrie. We'll be heading back there as soon as we run out of food."

The idea of camping on the claim for the summer and making no preparations for the future seemed odd to Reuben, but the Dugans' plan did set him to wondering. The ponies could pull the wagon, so might the Dugans sell the cow? As the question rose in his mind it was followed immediately by the knowledge that even if they were willing to sell, he had no money to buy. Nevertheless, before he headed back over the hill he broached the subject. "Sure I'd sell Pinky," Dugan said. "Of course cows are hard to get out here, so I'd want a good price, say ten dollars."

"Ten dollars," Reuben replied wistfully. "I'll think about it." But what he was really thinking once again was that for the price of the gun he could have a cow, and Ruth could have the milk she needed. But that was water under the bridge. The question now was where could he get ten dollars. He could try to sell the revolver, the only really portable thing he owned, but now the run was over there was likely little demand. Anybody who wanted a gun would want a rifle or a shotgun, something more practical for shooting game. Short of selling the pistol, what else could he do? "I'll think about it," he repeated, and bade the Dugans goodbye.

The Westerfields' sod house was built, but ten dollars, if they had it, would go a long way toward a proper roof, so even if they had the money, which would be the higher priority, a roof or a cow? They had little extra food to sell, even if there were buyers; besides what they traded to the Webers they would need all Ruth had stored for winter. What he did have were certain skills. He could play guitar and violin, and had even taught lessons, but trying to raise money in that way here seemed ludicrous. He was a carpenter, but the Weber house was finished, and he had traded work for the occasional use of the wagon and team. Nobody else within walking distance was building a house. Then there was blacksmithing. He had the tools and the skill to repair or make most anything that could be made of iron, and he'd thought all along that someday when there was demand he would supplement what he could make from farming with blacksmithing, perhaps even from carpentry and music as well.

But at the moment, he knew nobody who needed or would pay for anything he had to offer.

Reuben pondered the dilemma all the way home. As he came over the last rise and looked toward home he saw Ruth bent over the stove. She was feeding the firebox with another stick of wood. "That's it," he said aloud. "Firewood." Most of the trees along the Cimarron where they had gathered fuel were soft woods, cottonwood and willow. But he remembered that in the Gloss Mountains he'd seen both living and dead elm, hackberry, a scrubby oak of some sort and other trees he didn't recognize. There was lots of dead wood to be had, well-seasoned and ready to burn. He'd heard there were more than a hundred people in Okeene, so he could surely find a buyer. There was the hotel and saloon with a livery stable, a general store and now a scattering of houses and settler shacks. Winter would be coming soon, and there was almost no wood to be had on the plains. People would need fuel for heat in winter, and even in summer for cook stoves.

That evening Reuben and Ruth walked to the Weber house with a dozen eggs and arranged to borrow the wagon and team. Back home he sharpened his ax and gathered ropes. Before the next dawn he was up, the water and lunch Ruth had packed were loaded and he turned the team west once more toward the Gloss Mountains.

By late morning Reuben was in the hills and hard at work. He cut down half a dozen dead trees, chopped them into stove length and stacked the logs on the wagon. He worked on through the blazing afternoon heat, stopping only to eat and drink. When the sun sank low in the west he had a load. There would be no moon tonight, but he was just ten miles from town, and if he headed east he would sooner or later see its feeble lights. It was time to go, but perhaps he could pile on one more chopped up trunk before he tied down the load. He was busy calculating the value of his load, wondering if it might possibly bring ten dollars, thinking about strategies for selling, so preoccupied that he didn't hear the rattle until it was too late. The diamond back rattler sprang from its coil beside the fallen trunk and struck his left leg just above the boot. He brought down his ax and the snake was dead, but it was too late.

Reuben dropped to the log and tore off his boot. He rolled his pants leg, pulled out his bandana and tied it tight about his calf. He pulled out his pocket knife, opened the sharpest blade, and slit the flesh in an X across the already swelling bite. Fortunately it was on the inside of his calf, and with great difficulty he wrenched his leg high enough that he could reach it with his lips. He sucked venom and blood and spat, again and again. He rinsed his mouth, drank from his canteen and continued to suck. He pulled the tourniquet even tighter, quickly cinched his load, threw on his ax and pulled himself to the wagon seat. He lashed the horses with the reins and guided them east.

When the dim lights of Okeene came into view his vision was already blurred, and it took all his concentration to stay on the wagon seat and keep the team moving. Finally he turned up the dusty street and stopped the horses before the hotel. He slid off the wagon, tied the team and staggered to the door. The door screeched open and he collapsed on the floor.

The clerk looked up from behind the desk. "No drunks in here!" he yelled. He grabbed a night stick and headed for Reuben.

"I'm not drunk," Reuben stammered. "I'm snake-bit." Now the other man saw the dark naked foot and the sweat on Reuben's face.

"I'll get the doctor," he said, and he was out the door.

How long it took the doctor to arrive Reuben could not have told. But there was a blurry face above him, somebody pouring a fiery liquid into his mouth. Then they had him on a bed and were bathing his leg with cold water and massaging his foot. After a time the ceiling and the face above him came back into focus, and Reuben was able to mumble replies. They gave him more water, pulled a sheet up to his neck and turned out the lamp.

When he woke it was light. He looked around the strange room, and it slowly came to him how he happened to be here. He grasped the iron bedstead and pulled himself up. His leg was swollen and blue. The X he had cut was puffy and black. His head still swam in dizziness. He swung his legs to the floor, and grasping the frame, he stood. The left leg felt numb, but it seemed he might be able to walk. He saw his dungarees and right shoe beside the bed. The left shoe, he hoped, was still on the load. That reminded him of Weber's team. Were they still hitched outside?

Reuben pulled on his pants and the one sock and shoe and hobbled to the door and down the hall to the lobby. A new man was at the desk. "You must be the snake-bit guy," the clerk said. "I see you lived. Would you like a cup of coffee?"

"I guess I did," Reuben replied. "Yes, I'd like coffee."

"Oh, and by the way, here's your other shoe," the clerk said, pulling it from behind the desk. "The livery boy brought it in when he put your team away."

"Thanks," Reuben said, sipping hot coffee. "I need to be getting home. But I guess there will be some kind of bill to settle up?"

"Four dollars for the room and the team, and the doctor left his bill for five, which I can pass on to him. So nine dollars, all told."

Reuben swallowed the last sip and set the cup down. "I'm afraid I don't have any money," he said. "Neither with me nor at home. How much is a load of firewood worth?"

The clerk studied Reuben for a moment, probably trying to gauge whether his claim of poverty was true. "Well, in that case, I guess a load of firewood would be worth about nine dollars," he said. "We'll need some in the hotel, and I'll settle up with the doctor. But you're in no shape to work. I'll have the livery boy unload it in back and hitch your team."

"Thank you," was all Reuben could manage. He had endured a day of back-breaking work and a rattlesnake bite, and now he would go home, not only empty-handed, but likely unable to accomplish much for several days. He pulled on his other sock and shoe, leaving it unlaced, and hobbled out. He was not just back to square one, but now he didn't even have a plan. Unless he thought of something else, they would face the winter with a leaking roof, and the only cow in the neighborhood would be out of reach. It was a long ride back to the homestead.

CHAPTER 16

July passed, then August, and rain refused to fall. Days were hot, often over a hundred degrees. Both the dugout and the sod house remained tolerably cool, but the only shade was the scattering of trees at the edge of the bluff and by the spring and along the creek. Often they packed a lunch and walked to the spring, where they cooled themselves in the gurgling water that faithfully flowed, even as the hard red soil cracked in the sun. Hobbling on his snake-bit leg for weeks before it began to feel strong again, Reuben carried buckets of water every day to the garden, to the fruit trees and to the cottonwood they had transplanted west of the soddy. But no amount of water artificially applied makes up for a lack of rain; the drying earth quickly absorbed whatever water he brought. The garden was shriveling, though there were still potatoes, onions and carrots in the ground. The transplanted trees had not lost their leaves, but neither had they grown. Just keeping things alive in the worsening drought was a challenge.

Ruth's pregnancy was now five months advanced. Even with the hard work of gardening, canning and cooking, her appetite in the oppressive heat was weak. Reuben saw that as her belly swelled, her face seemed ever more gaunt. She needed better nutrition, meat and milk. Meat he could supply occasionally, but that too was a challenge. He had just one dwindling box of shells for the revolver, and he had not learned to shoot well, at least not well enough to consistently kill a rabbit or a prairie chicken with the revolver, and he could not hope to take down a deer. He fashioned a trap and placed it between the garden and the spring and did catch an occasional cottontail rabbit, and once a big jackrabbit that required long simmering on the stove before it was tender enough to eat.

Reuben's plan to acquire a milk cow had failed, but now he felt he might be well enough to make another try. This time he'd be watching and listening every moment for snakes. It would be blazing hot to chop wood, but if he could get another load and sell it, maybe he could still buy the Dugans' cow. If he tilled the garden plants that were still alive and added more mulch to hold the moisture, perhaps he could take a day off from watering and make another trip to the hills. He would walk over to Webers after supper and see if he could borrow the team.

While they were eating lunch under the big willow by the spring they heard voices to the west. Presently the Dugans topped the rise, the two paints plodding along before the wagon, the family riding in the shade of the tattered canopy. Pinky the Jersey cow trailed behind. Reuben jumped to his feet and waved. Rupert turned the team toward the spring and pulled them to a halt.

"Well, it's time for us to head back to Guthrie," Rupert announced. "But we might refill our water jug from your spring if that's OK."

"Be our guest," Reuben said. The family climbed down from the wagon, the kids looking dirtier and more ragged than ever, and joined the Westerfields in the shade. While Rupert submerged the jug in the pool below the spring, Reuben shared his plan to go back to the hills for another load of wood, which he anticipated he could sell for ten dollars and buy the cow. "So we'd like to buy Pinky if we could," Reuben ventured. "I should be able to have the money in a couple of days, if you could camp here and wait."

"I'm afraid we couldn't do that," Rupert said. "We're pretty much out of food, and the in-laws will be expecting us. I have to find some kind of work in Guthrie or we'll starve this winter."

"We can give you food," Ruth offered. "We still have potatoes and squash and a few tomatoes in the garden, and still plenty of eggs."

"Oh, I'm afraid we couldn't impose on you," Rupert replied, obviously eager to be off.

"Well, in that case, maybe I could find a way to get the money to you," Reuben ventured. "I could walk to Hennessey and find somebody to take it down on the train."

Rupert looked skeptical. He was likely reluctant to turn over the cow to a man he barely knew, a man who after a whole summer of work still couldn't come up with ten dollars. "Well, I thank you for the offer and for the water, but I think we'd best keep the cow and be on our way," he said. "Anyway, she'll be going dry before long, and we need to get her bred. That's something you couldn't do out here, unless of course you wanted to turn over the calf as payment to the man with the only bull in the country."

"Somebody has a bull?" Reuben asked in surprise.

"Sure, you haven't met Arden Breedlove?" Rupert said. "He has a high class bull and a big roan stud. He was in the saloon in Okeene, playing cards and buying drinks for everybody and offering his services, five bucks a throw, or in the case of a cow, five bucks or turn over the calf when it's born."

"A big roan stud, you say?" Reuben asked. "A dark roan? Did the man have a scar across his cheek?"

"That would be the man," Rupert replied. "He's your neighbor, actually. Lives in a shack not far beyond my place. That would be about four miles west of here. If you've been to Okeene you've passed his place. Second little rise past our claim, long slant of grass sloping south, little stream in the far corner. Well, we got a long way to go. Back in the wagon, kids. We'd best be on our way." And with that the family tumbled back into the wagon and creaked away, the big-eyed Jersey's teats swinging rhythmically side to side. Ruth and Reuben watched wistfully until they disappeared over the ridge.

Across the Cimarron

CHAPTER 17

Another month passed, and Ruth's belly continued to grow. But in spite of work in the summer sun she seemed not only gaunt but pale. Reuben reluctantly left her for a day and drove Peter's team back to the Gloss Mountains for another load of wood. He passed at a distance the place that must be Arden Breedlove's claim. So that was his name. Just passing the place made Reuben nervous. It was likely that sooner or later they would meet, but he wasn't eager. On the other hand, if they ever got a cow the time might come that he would need to have her bred. He cut another load of wood, which with winter approaching he was able to sell at the hotel. In the hills he also found sheets of thin translucent selenite to place in the window openings of the soddy for a little winter light.

So now they had ten dollars and change in a jar, but there was no cow to buy. He thought of walking to Hennessey to see if he could find one there. Or should he buy ten dollars worth of lumber and patch together a solid roof? If he spent the money either way, they'd be broke if Ruth needed the doctor in Okeene.

There was one other option, one he refused to even contemplate—mortgage the land. It wasn't exactly legal to mortgage a claim that you hadn't proved up on, but he'd heard in town about a card shark who was meeting settlers in the saloon and offering fifteen dollars for the papers on their claims. If the settler paid back the money within a year, plus interest, he would get the papers back. If not, the lender would take the claim. Apparently a couple of desperate homesteaders had already mortgaged their claims to get the cash to hang on, but for Reuben that would be an absolute last resort. Clearly his prospects looked as risky as that of any gambler. Even if it rained and he got a crop next June, wheat prices might drop even further. But the land was all they had, and even if nothing looked promising at the moment, if they were to have a future it must be on this land.

He pondered these choices as he broke up hard earth by hand in the ten acres he had plowed. They had now waited all summer and through September for a good rain, but the rain hadn't come. There was a shower at the end of the month, but not enough to germinate seed. If they didn't get a good soaking soon, the wheat might not get established before the weather turned cold. Or worse yet, they might get a little shower that would sprout the ill-planted seeds, only to have them wither as new roots reached for moisture that wasn't there. But now it was October, and he had to play his hand. If he waited any longer it would be too late to plant.

The other thing that occupied his mind was the pistol. He knew deep down that without it they might not have this place with its life-preserving spring, but he couldn't escape the gnawing notion that the purchase had been foolish. If he was going to buy a gun, he at least should have bought a rifle or a shotgun, something useful for taking prairie chickens, turkeys, rabbits and deer, all of which were still fairly abundant along the river. He often saw deer drinking from their creek in early mornings. If he could kill a deer, at least they would have meat for the winter.

He tried not to let Ruth see, but Reuben was crazy with worry. If he walked to Hennessey, there was no guarantee he could find a cow to buy, especially not for ten dollars. Possibly he could sell the pistol, or trade for a cow, or at least a rifle or a shotgun, but these were all long shots. He could see himself returning after a two-day walk with nothing to show for his time but sore feet. That would also mean leaving Ruth alone for two days. Though he saw that she also tried to hide her condition from him, he knew that she often felt weak and even ill. Clearly she wasn't getting the nourishment that a woman with child should have.

One reason he was reluctant to leave her was that Peter had heard in Okeene that a small band of young Arapahos were camping down the Cimarron, unhappy about their land being diminished and broken up by allotments, and by the fact that settlers had been cutting down trees and shooting the deer and other game. More than once Ruth and Reuben had seen moccasin prints by the spring. The most alarming thing Weber had heard, which neither he nor Reuben told their wives, was that a settler a few miles down the river had shot a young Indian, and that the Arapahos at Cantonment were plotting revenge. Thus was Reuben's mind preoccupied as he broadcasted his precious wheat seed. There were so many more immediate things to worry about that he thought less about whether the seed would grow.

After several days of backbreaking work, he had sewn ten acres with seed and raked it in. In the corner nearest the house he planted a patch of turnips. If they did well they would produce a great quantity of winter food. Now if it would only rain. Two days after he finished planting, Reuben was dragging the cook stove into the soddy and hooking up the chimney pipe when a dark cloud came boiling up in the western sky. Just as he finished the job and brought in an armful of wood, a northwest wind collided with the southerly wind, and a powerful thunderstorm erupted across the prairie. Ruth and Reuben watched out the little south window as the willows and cottonwoods by the spring swayed and swooped, then watched the gusts move across the prairie grasses, bending them low to the ground, saw a great cloud of dust rise from the wheat field and swim across the sky, heard the tempest pass overhead, jerking and tearing at the tarpaulin roof, and finally moving off down the bluff to churn the water of the Cimarron and rock the trees on its banks. Then the sky grew dark and the rain poured down.

Water dripped through the roof in several places, mostly minor leaks, but winter had not yet begun. They moved the bed from its corner and watched the trickle of water splash on the grassy floor. Reuben built a fire in the stove, Ruth put on a kettle of water for coffee, and soon they were warm inside and out, watching the storm play itself out, confident that at least now the wheat would sprout. For the first time in months Reuben dragged his fiddle out of the chest, tuned it up and played.

If the summer had been brutal and dry, fall was brief before the first snow flew. Surely this was unusual, they thought, to have a blizzard before Thanksgiving! The wheat and turnips were up, and the snow brought more moisture, but most of the snow blew off the open ground and drifted around the trees and the little house. They had enough food stored in the house and in the dugout to last the winter, so they were sure they wouldn't starve. But for months there would be nothing fresh, except perhaps turnip greens. Meat was still scarce, and Ruth had had no milk in seven months of pregnancy. It looked like a long winter ahead.

Sitting by the open door of the stove that evening, Ruth and Reuben discussed whether it might still be possible to get back to Wichita for the winter. They finally concluded that Ruth couldn't walk the twenty miles to Hennessey, and even if they got there, she certainly couldn't hop a freight. It would take most of the money they had for two passenger tickets. Furthermore, her parents weren't exactly flush. Of course they would take the young couple in, and somehow would stretch what they had, and Ruth knew that they would be relieved and delighted to have them back from the frontier. But like all the other choices they faced, this one did not seem wise, to spend all they had to go crawling home and admit defeat.

In the end they saw no real option besides sticking it out. But with little work that he could do now, Reuben did begin to think more seriously about a trip to Hennessey, or wherever he might have to go to sell the pistol, or perhaps trade it for a more practical gun. If Ruth couldn't have milk, at least he should provide meat.

CHAPTER 18

They were digging the last of the potatoes and the first of the turnips, he spading and she gathering tubers into a gunny sack, when they heard a rifle shot somewhere on Spring Creek. Reuben dropped the shovel and ran to the house for the Colt. If somebody was shooting on his place they'd better have a good reason. He emerged from the house and strode across the prairie toward the grove.

"Reuben, be careful," Ruth called. "I don't think you should go up there. What if it's an Indian, or an outlaw of some kind?"

"Don't worry, I can take care of myself," he said. "I'll be back soon."

He approached the spring cautiously, the revolver in his hand. Most of the underbrush had yet to lose its leaves, so all he could make out was some sort of movement until he was very close. When he came to the clearing, what he saw was an Indian man, a man somewhat older than himself, his braids peppered with gray, crouched over a fallen deer. He watched in silence for a moment, anger rising in his throat. Ruth desperately needed better nutrition, and here this stranger had killed a deer at his spring on his land.

At last he spoke. "What are you doing on my land?" he called out. The other man looked up, startled, but did not reply. His rifle lay beside him in the grass. He had slit the deer's throat and now squatted with his hand on its nose, mumbling something Reuben could not understand.

Reuben advanced toward the man, his pistol raised. "What are you doing shooting a deer on my land?" he demanded again.

The Indian glanced up again from whatever it was he was doing. When he saw the gun pointed at him he slowly rose. In the man's eyes Reuben saw not fear, but something like defiance. The man spoke again, words that to Reuben had no meaning.

"This is my deer," Reuben said. "You have shot it without my permission and on my land."

The man stepped past the deer and advanced toward Reuben, leaving his rifle on the ground. When he was close he extended his hand. "I am Watongah," he said. "Black Coyote in English. I know your tongue. I was interpreter for government agent Miles ten winters back—before he lied to our chiefs and leased our land to a rancher name George Reynolds for two cents an acre, all the land from Cantonment to Fort Reno, all the land a man could walk in two days."

"But what does that have to do with me?" Reuben asked. "This is my land. You can't hunt on my land without my permission, which I did not give."

"Yes, the government says this is your land," the other replied, dropping his extended hand. "Since I was a young man I have hunted this land. Now the government has pushed us to a corner of our land and there are ten white men for every Cheyenne or Arapaho. You have most of our land, but my people are hungry, and I killed this deer for them."

Reuben hesitated, not sure what to do. The man seemed not only fearless, but harmless. Slowly he lowered the Colt, shifted it to his left hand, and extended his own hand. "My name is Reuben," he said. "My wife and I live in the house over there. We also need meat for winter, but you have killed a deer on our Spring Creek."

Black Coyote smiled. "You have claimed this land, but you don't know this land. This is not Spring Creek. Spring Creek flows to the salt creek an hour's walk west. I know this land. My people have held ceremonies by this spring for many summers."

Not Spring Creek? Maybe the Indian was right. Maybe the name had already been claimed by somebody else. But he had used that name for his own life-sustaining creek long enough that it was firmly fixed in his mind. To him, Spring Creek it would remain. But that was not the point. This was his land!

Now Black Coyote raised his own hand again and lightly took Reuben's. The Indian's hand was at least as hard and rough as his. Reuben slipped free, his indignation returning. "Whatever this creek is called, it's mine now," he said. "Your people were given allotments before the white people came."

"Allotments," Black Coyote repeated, as if reciting once again a story he had told too many times before. "We did not ask for allotments. We wanted to live as we always have lived. Your chiefs in Washington forced us to this reservation in 1875. Then white men killed the buffalo for hide and bone and our people starved. In ten years half were dead. The government gave us skinny cows, never enough. They took our children for their schools, they took our religion, they wanted us be farmers, fence off land, to sell Mother Earth. They drove us apart, put our chiefs in jail. They cut rations. Children and grandmothers starved."

"But didn't the government pay the Cheyenne and Arapaho for this land?" Reuben cut in. "I read this in the newspaper."

"One dollar an acre," Black Coyote said, seeming now to grow impatient, as if with an inattentive pupil. "But our land was not for sale. Our chiefs said no. Our men said no. Agents threatened old women and children, made them sign. They didn't buy the land. They stole the land."

"But the government let you pick your allotments before white people came in," Reuben insisted. "Your people got the best land, the river valleys, the best timber in the country."

"Yes, and now white men come with wagons and cut the trees and haul them away to build houses and barns. When the trees go the deer go too."

Reuben's head was spinning. If what Black Coyote said was true, did he really have a right to this land? Was this water really his. And this deer? He became aware of the revolver dangling from his left hand. He reached behind him and pushed the weapon into his belt. But what should he do now? He dare not try to throw the Indian off the land by force, and the other's argument was strong. What if all he said was true? Reuben was silent now, staring at the gurgling spring and at the deer at Black Coyote's feet.

"I give you half," Black Coyote said suddenly. From his back pocket he withdrew a coil of braded rope. He slipped it around the deer's back hooves and drew the loop tight. He pulled a long knife from his belt and laid it beside his rifle on the ground. He motioned for Reuben to help.

As if awaking from a trance, Reuben moved toward the deer. The Indian threw the rope over a cottonwood limb and pulled it taut. Reuben grasped the doe in front of the flanks and lifted, and soon the deer swung from the branch, blood still seeping from its throat and mouth. Black Coyote made long swift slits down each leg and down the belly from tail to neck, then the knife glided deftly between skin and flesh, and soon the hide slid off onto the grass. Black Coyote rolled it into a bundle and tied it with another scrap of rope. He inserted the razor sharp knife into the belly and spilled the guts, then the knife plunged into the spine and split the carcass into equal halves. Black Coyote washed blood from his hands and the knife in the spring, slung his rifle across his back, directed Reuben to take one hind hoof while he took the other, and cut the carcass down.

Half an hour after he'd heard the rifle shot Reuben still stood in the little clearing, listening to the gurgle of the spring, but now with his pistol in his belt and half a deer draped over his back. "Thank you," he said, as the Indian shouldered his half, touched Reuben's hand again, and walked west.

Until Black Coyote passed out of sight over the ridge, Reuben stood transfixed. He realized he had no idea where the other man lived. Surely it was not many miles away, if he could carry the heavy load home. He wanted to call out and ask, but it was too late. Blinking away what seemed like a dream, he turned and trudged toward the house with the heavy load of flesh and bone on his back. The weather was already turning colder, so they could cut up the meat and dry it for winter, no need for canning. They would have no milk, but they would have all the vegetables and meat they would need.

CHAPTER 19

Ruth still sprawled across Reuben's legs, her eyes open but dull and glazed. In her line of vision, if she was aware, lay a long stretch of swirling muddy water between their flotsam raft and the western bank. Every kind of debris bobbed on the roiling surface, bits of lumber, none of which ever drifted close enough to grab, scraps of buildings, bales of hay, bottles and cans. Scanning the river and registering these objects, Reuben's eyes fell on what looked like a saddle. Sure enough, a saddled horse was floating by. Had it borne a rider, and if so what had happened to that person, he wondered. His back and legs were cramped and stiff from clinging to the slanted roof in the cold rain, his buttocks numb from hours without moving. He wanted to stand and stretch, but that was not possible on the slippery slope. He was reluctant to move at all, since any movement would disturb Ruth's rest, peaceless though it might be.

He stroked her arm, but she did not respond. What a wonder, how familiar this body was, hair now white and matted by rain, but arms, legs and body still slender, and still strong for eighty-seven. Her breasts had never been large, and now there was hardly a bulge beneath her dress. Even when Jacob was born her breasts had never been full, partly because of her slender frame, but also because her body lacked what it needed to produce much milk.

He recalled their first Christmas on the claim. He had cut a little cedar by Salt Creek and Ruth decorated it with bright buttons and bows. They had nothing to put under the tree, but Ruth made a special dinner, a venison roast and vegetables. The sun was bright in the afternoon, and they walked to the Cimarron and nestled together in a thick clump of grass. The baby was now just weeks, or maybe even days away. Reuben wasn't sure Ruth should expend the energy for a long walk, but she insisted the exercise and sun would do her good.

About mid afternoon the wind shifted to the northwest and clouds rolled in. The couple rose from their nest and started back up the bluff. Half way up Ruth began to feel faint, then she fell and seemed unable to get up. Reuben picked her up, cradled her in his arms and trudged up the hill against the wind to the house. He laid her on the bed and brought her some water. Soon she felt better, but seemed to lack the strength, and perhaps the will, to get up from bed. Reuben decided that whatever the cost, he must take her to Okeene to the doctor, and try to buy some milk.

When Ruth seemed comfortable he ran across the hills to the Webers' place. He and Peter readied the team and wagon and he drove back for her. By now the sky was growing dark, not only from the shortness of the day, but from heavy clouds. They put on their warmest clothes and heavy coats and set out into the wind.

Reuben watched to the left of the trail, and thought he saw what must be Breedlove's shack. Then snow began to fall, driven into their faces by the wind. Besides their heavy coats Reuben had brought the blankets from the bed. These he wrapped around Ruth and made her as comfortable as possible on the wagon bed behind the seat, where his body blocked some of the wind and snow.

Soon the whole landscape was white, and Reuben's only clue to the trail was a crooked line worn through the sea of bowing prairie grass. He drove straight into the stinging blast, his eyes open just enough to be sure the horses didn't stray off the path, where everything would look the same and they would surely be lost. But concentration on this single task could not hold off worry and fear. He tried not to think about Ruth and the baby, but driving into this December blast brought a new worry to his mind. Would his late-planted and barely-rooted wheat freeze out? His crop was up, spotty of course, as one would expect with hand-broadcast seed, but a little rain in the fall had given him hope for a decent harvest. But even if the seedlings didn't freeze, if they survived and grew, and then after the work of harvesting and threshing by hand, hauling the wheat to town and paying freight on the train, if the price dropped any further, would anything be left? In the blizzard it was hard to remember the summer's drought, but he knew it was deep. If next spring's rainfall was like 1892, would he even get a crop?

For an hour they labored into the storm, an hour in which feeble light faded to snowy dusk, and at last the even more feeble lights of Okeene came into view. He drove to the hotel and asked where the doctor might be found. "The doctor's house is the one with paint at the north end of the street," the clerk said. Reuben went back out into the storm and turned the horses north.

The doctor's wife opened the door. They were just finishing supper, but the doctor came immediately and took Ruth to a bed for examination. She was very pale, and her pulse was weak, her eyes sunken in gaunt cheeks. "I find nothing wrong with this woman except that she appears malnourished," the doctor said when his examination was complete. "Has she had plenty of protein and milk?"

"No milk, I'm afraid," Reuben replied guiltily. Somehow he should have been able to supply what she needed, though he knew the failure was not for lack of trying. "She has had plenty of vegetables and meat."

"It appears to me that the baby might be a week or two away," the doctor said. "In the meantime, she should drink all the milk she can, and rest. That's all we can do."

Reuben paid the five dollar fee, and they went back out into the howling storm. Returning home was out of the question now. They would have to spend four dollars on a hotel room and livery stable, which would leave them a dollar and change. When Ruth was settled in bed, Reuben went back to the desk to ask where he might buy milk. The clerk directed him to a house on the south edge of town where a family he knew had a cow. The next problem was that Reuben had no container for milk. The hotel man loaned him a jar, and while the livery boy unhitched and fed the team, Reuben found the shack at the other end of the street and bought milk.

"Could I buy more tomorrow morning to take home?" he asked. "And would you have something you could loan to take it in, something I would return, but not right away?" The woman found an old bucket and washed it out and promised to fill it when she milked the next morning.

Ruth seemed revived by the cool milk, and they slept. In the morning they had a little bread at the hotel lobby and Reuben hitched the team. By sun up they were at the milk woman's door, where Reuben paid a dollar for the bucket of milk, which the woman covered with a scrap of oil cloth. The snow was deep enough that it came over his shoe tops, and once they left town they found the trail laced with drifts deep as the wagon's axle. But the blizzard was over and the horses plodded steadily through the drifts, east into the rising sun.

Reuben took Ruth and the precious milk into the house, built a hot fire in the stove and returned Weber's team. He walked back home in the wagon track where the horses had broken the crust through drifts. When he entered the house the air was humid. What Ruth had discovered while he was gone was that the heat had melted snow on the roof, which had dripped through onto their bed and on most everything else in the house. Weak as she was, Ruth had removed the covers and draped them across the chairs to dry. Now there was nothing more to do but keep the fire blazing so Ruth would be warm and could rest and wait for the baby to come. Perhaps by bedtime the blankets would be dry.

Reuben acted as cheerful as he could, and he even brought out the guitar and played a couple of songs. But in truth he was a knot of worry. There was Ruth's frailty, the question of whether proper nutrition at this late date would help, the fact that once the bucket of milk was gone there would be no more, the even more troubling fact that their savings now jingled as a few coins in his pocket. On top of all that, the hotel clerk had told him the news from a Chicago paper. Several banks had gone broke across the country, and thousands of men were out of work. Worst of all for him, wheat had dropped another twenty cents a bushel.

It would be a long winter, no doubt. There would be little to occupy his mind, little work to be done besides trying to keep the roof patched and the rain out, keeping the firewood pile high and a blaze in the stove. All they could do was wait for the baby and what an uncertain future might bring. Reuben drove a nail outside the door post where he could hang the bucket high when the weather was above freezing. When it was colder they would set it just inside the door.

Each day Ruth seemed a little stronger, with more color in her cheeks. The baby was kicking in her womb, and she let Reuben feel. It was reassuring, this strong evidence of life. "But there's no telling when the baby will come," Ruth said. "I don't know whether it's more important to keep drinking the milk now, or save it until after the birth."

"We have just over a gallon left," Reuben replied. "If you continue to drink a pint each day, it will last a little over a week. Surely the baby will be here by then. And anyway, I don't know how long it will keep." Ruth agreed to the plan.

On the tenth of January, Ruth awoke before dawn with labor pains. The wind had howled all night, and when Reuben lighted the lamp he saw a little pyramid of snow on either side of the door. A dusting of snow had filtered through cracks and settled on the table. He built up the fire, put water on to boil for coffee, put on all the warmest clothes he had and opened the door to find snow half way up the door. He thrashed his way through the drift and plunged into darkness toward the Weber house. He wanted Esther here in case the birth came soon. He was pretty sure that Esther had no particular knowledge of childbirth; she'd told Ruth that she had never witnessed a birth. Yet it seemed necessary to have another woman in the house, and indeed Esther had been firm in her insistence that when the time came, he should come for her. Surely she could offer something that Reuben would not know how to give.

Reuben had trudged only a few dozen steps south when he realized that he'd already left all bearings behind. There was a faint light in the east, so he was pretty sure he was walking south, but beyond that, the entire world looked the same. It was a world of churning white, of drifts and valleys without end, he a desolate speck sandwiched between the white at his feet and the swirling white of the sky. He paused and looked back. The sod walls of the house had already disappeared! What should he do? He feared returning to Ruth without Esther, feared he would not have the slightest idea what to expect, what the next few hours might bring, what he might be called upon to do that he would not know how to do. Fear was not familiar to Reuben, but he was alarmed now at the depth of panic he felt, alarm not only about Ruth, but about the tender being he would hold in his two coarse hands.

Reuben faced west, and the icy blast stung his cheeks. If the wind continued to blow from the west and the light continued to grow in the east, he should be able to pick his way over the rise and down again to the Weber house, then reverse his footsteps with Esther in tow. He looked back at his tracks, and saw that they were already drifting closed. He realized with shock that there would be no trail to follow. What if the snow became even heavier, the wind more furious? What if he made it to the Webers' but they couldn't find their way back? Or what if he lost his way and missed their house, where at this hour there would still be no light?

Snow swirled around his feet. Ice was forming in his mustache as his breath melted snow. His eyes stung as if he were facing a raging fire. He stood for a minute more, not moving his feet, considering options and the possible outcomes of plunging ahead, or turning back. The one scenario that would not leave his head was the image of Ruth alone in the soddy, the fire burning low, Ruth screaming in pain, nobody there to hold her hand or put wood in the stove while he wandered lost in a driving blizzard, or worse yet, frozen in a snow bank from which he would never return home.

At last Reuben turned his feet back the way he had come, the biting snow now defining direction by its assault on his left cheek rather than his right. In the moments he had deliberated, his tracks were nearly obliterated! He plunged blindly back toward what he thought was north. Then in a momentary easing of the wind he made out the brown of sod walls. From inside the house he heard a low wail that rose to a cry. He staggered to the door, let himself in and tugged the door closed against the storm. He dropped to his knees beside the bed. "I couldn't find my way," he whimpered. He grasped Ruth's hot hand in his cold hands and brought it to his icy lips. "I was afraid I'd be lost and then there would be nobody to help," he explained. "We'll have to do this alone, just you and me."

In answer Ruth arched her back and cried out again through clenched teeth. She couldn't speak in words, but words would have been of little use. Reuben clutched her tight in his arms, his eyes madly searching the interior of the room, looking for the things he might need, and for answers to questions he could not define. Now water was bubbling over the pot and splashing on the hot stove. Reuben released Ruth and stood. He had to calm himself. He had heard women, his mother and others, talk of childbirth. He must think clearly and do what had to be done.

He gathered the cleanest towels and rags he could find. He folded two towels under Ruth and lay the others on the bed at her feet. The rags he dropped into the bubbling pot. He pulled one from the water with a fork, and when it had cooled a moment, scrubbed his calloused hands. He dipped a tin platter into the pot, one side then the other, and laid it on the stove beside the pot. He took the butcher knife from the shelf, held the steel in the water, then laid it alongside hot rags on the platter. He couldn't think of anything else to do, so he returned to Ruth's side to hold her hand and wait.

The wait was long. He stroked her cheek and wiped perspiration from her brow. First she was hot, then cold. She stifled cries as best she could, but her pain came in waves, waves that she rode until they broke, then plunged into the valley to wait for the next crest to rise. At last it came to Reuben that neither of them had had anything to eat, or even to drink. He got up and brought the dipper of water to Ruth's lips. Then he dipped boiling water into a smaller pot, chopped some dried venison and turnips and threw them in to boil. When it was softened to soup he brought a bowl to Ruth. She wouldn't eat, but between contractions she took small sips of the hot broth. And then, as if the liquid primed a pump, her water broke and the towels below her hips were soaked.

Reuben changed the towels, ate what he could and waited. The light through the cracks grew stronger, though the sun was blocked by the howling storm. The day wore on, marked by rhythmic moans of pain, and then the streaks of light again grew dim. Reuben left Ruth's side, opened the door and peered out. The bleak light was fading, so Ruth's labor had worn on for ten hours or more, and still the baby had not come. With falling darkness the wind and snow were subsiding. He stepped outside. He could see the woods that marked the river now, and squinting southwest he made out the slender trunks of the fruit trees they had planted. Now it might be possible to go for Esther. Perhaps he could be there and return in half an hour. But night was falling fast, and Ruth's pains seemed ever more intense. Surely the time was near, and what if he went for Esther now, and before they returned the baby should come? He gazed into the world of white, but found no answers. At last he pulled the door shut and knelt again by the bed. Going for Esther was a risk he couldn't take.

The next time Reuben glanced toward the door, no light was visible through the cracks. And now Ruth's moans had become screams. And then her hips raised high and she gave a mighty cry and a tiny head appeared. Reuben's hands went instinctively to her belly and gently stroked, as if to massage the baby into the world. And little by little it came. Reuben dipped more rags into the simmering pot and remembered again to wash his hands, then rung the rags dry and stroked her heaving belly. At last a mighty thrust and a gasping form was expelled, a baby boy so small it little more than filled the palm of his hand.

With the other hand he mopped slimy liquid from the tiny face. He wrapped the now squalling baby in a warm towel. He reached for the knife and deftly sliced the cord and tied a knot. He handed their son to Ruth and began to clean the mess.

Soon the baby's shrill howls diminished to a whimper, and then were still. Reuben rushed back to Ruth's side and laid a big palm across the baby's belly and chest. Yes, he was breathing. Reuben finished the cleaning, then brought Ruth another cup of steaming broth. Now she too was quiet. She lay limp on the bed, the baby clutched against her breast. For a time, both mother and infant seemed to sleep. Reuben gathered what had collected on the towels, opened the door and flung it to the wind. He threw all the wet and soiled things into a pot, added more water and put more wood in the stove. Now it was so warm and humid in the room that he was sweating. He took off his clothes down to his undershirt. While mother and baby slept, he wolfed down turnips and venison, then knelt again by the bed. For the first time he felt the leisure to admire his son.

Ruth's eyes opened, and Reuben kissed her lips. "You've done a wonderful thing, my love," he said. "You have brought us a son." He reached and took the small bundle into his hands again. They of course had no scale, but compared to other babies he had seen, he guessed the boy might weigh five pounds.

"Shall we call him Jacob?" Ruth said weakly. "To remember your father?"

"That would be wonderful," Reuben agreed. "My father would like nothing better. I wish he could see his grandson."

As if he knew they were talking about him, the tiny, wrinkled baby opened his eyes, and immediately began a feeble cry. Ruth opened her dress and put his lips to her small breast. He fussed and cried until his face was red, but seemed unable to drink. Reuben remembered that they had a small jar of the milk left, now more than two weeks old, but since they had kept it cool, it had not soured. He retrieved the jar, poured the contents into a small pan and set it on the stove. He had no idea where the next milk might come from, but for now Ruth would have one last drink that he hoped might spur her own milk, milk that Jacob would desperately need.

Across the Cimarron

CHAPTER 20

Reuben wondered how much time had passed. The river raged here and rolled there, depending on what the waters encountered below, but the progress of the chicken house, always slow, was mostly steady. Now and then it bumped against some obstacle, jolted gently and backed up water, producing a reverse wake that lapped over the lower edge of the roof. Then the building slowly turned to free itself and continued its course.

If only he had a long pole, he might be able to nudge the craft out of the current and toward shore, and perhaps eventually they'd run aground in water shallow enough and close enough that they could try for land. But land was far away, sometimes a quarter mile, usually more, he judged. The current bore them continuously down the old river channel, the deepest water, and there was no reason to think the pattern would change.

Reuben became aware of the hollowness of his stomach, aware that for some time it had rumbled and churned, a sensation he had felt but had not heard over the rain and wind. He realized they had not eaten since last night's supper, and though the sun was not in evidence, it must be past noon. No doubt the weariness he felt, and the more alarming weakness apparent in Ruth's prostrate figure, was partly from lack of food. No use dwelling on that. There was nothing to be had. Neither had they had anything to drink in all those hours, and his throat was parched. He cupped his hands and held them together for some minutes until they had accumulated a small swallow of water and poured it into his mouth. He repeated the process, nudged Ruth awake from her stupor and emptied his hands into her mouth.

Besides wet and cold, hunger and thirst and the numbness and ache of every muscle and joint in his body, there was growing fatigue. He craved rest. But what if he should fall asleep and the roof should tip and dump them into the river, or perhaps worse, what if the opportunity to gain shore presented itself and he was not aware. Reuben scanned the western horizon, which consisted of muddy water below and dark skies and rain above with a vague ribbon of land between. But as he watched, the rain appeared to be slackening; the river banks seemed to be gaining a sharper outline. They had passed the region where the high bluff formed the western bank, so they must have floated down the river something like six or seven miles. That would put them somewhere in the river bottom neighborhood south of where Bertram and Sally had settled, and where their son Tom and his wife Betsy now lived. He scanned the low horizon for a landmark.

The lingering tinge of guilt he had never been able to fully dispel clouded Reuben's mind, as it always did when he thought of Bertram. It was true that they were in no position to help Bertram and Sally when they showed up that first spring. They had their own burdens then, and their own sorrow, not only the daily struggle to survive, but also the terrible loss which haunted every waking moment, the loss from which he believed Ruth had never fully recovered. He had been in no position to give Bertram land or money or even advice, or at summer's end even food, but he could have given Bertram what he perhaps needed most, simple acknowledgement. Instead on that first morning, had it not been for Ruth's intervention, he was prepared to turn Bertram and Sally away, sending them off to survive as best they could in a place that was proving far more difficult to survive in than he had ever imagined, even for a white man. But for a black man who arrived after the free land was gone, nearly impossible.

Through long years of abject poverty as itinerant hired hands, their life had been little better than the life of slavery their forebears had known. Yet Bertram and Sally had survived. Reuben knew that was testament to an inner strength deeper even than his own, a determination spawned of their knowledge that the only alternative to survival was to not survive. Despite their harsh struggle Bertram and Sally had endured, had found a place of their own, and after twenty years of hard work and often doing without were able to add good farm land, river bottom land that was better than the high plain where Reuben had homesteaded. On that place they had thrived, and long before Bertram and Sally went to their graves they had passed the farm to their only son, Tom. Tom, who himself was now grown old, had added more land and had become a prominent farmer and a leader in the small community of Negroes founded by those who'd come in search of something to call their own.

Straining his eyes to the west he made out what looked like a windmill just above the water line. And yes, behind that a big red barn. Could that be Tom's place? Yes, it had to be! His arm involuntarily rose and he began to wave and shout, though his voice was dry and hoarse. Now he made out cows at the tank beside the windmill. If by chance Tom or Betsy was outside perhaps they would hear him, or see his frantic waves. After all these hours, the rain was now a mere drizzle, and they and their lifeboat must be visible from land. If somebody heard him or happened to look their way, it was possible they might be noticed and saved.

Reuben waved and shouted for as long as he thought it possible for somebody to hear or see, but the raft floated slowly on, dragging sluggishly through the rushing water, and finally the distance between them and the windmill had grown wide. At least his waving and hoarse shouts revived Ruth. She struggled to raise up from his legs. "Where are we now?" she asked feebly. He heard in her voice not only growing weakness, but also that her throat was raw.

"We've just passed Tom and Betsy's place," Reuben said. "That would put us a few miles west of Dover."

"We're going to die out here," Ruth said flatly. "I wish we could at least have died at home."

"Don't even think that," Reuben replied in a voice that exuded far more confidence than he felt. "We've been through worse than this," he said, then realized that he had probably opened the old wound again. "We've been through everything life could dish out," he quickly added, "hunger, drought, grasshoppers, and now fire and flood on the same night. But don't worry. We'll get out of this river. See how the rain has let up? Before you know it the sun will be out and somebody will spot us and come with a boat to get us off. You just rest. We're going to be all right."

"No, we're not going to be rescued," Ruth asserted. "I just wish we could have died at home. We could have been buried on our land, next to Jacob, instead of being lost in this muddy water and never even found."

"Please don't talk like that," Reuben said. "I'll get us out, I swear I will. Surely we can get off the river when we come to the bridge south of Dover. No doubt there will be a way to get out there. We'll go home and we'll rebuild, just as we've done before." Now Ruth was silent, having pronounced the end, and Reuben was left to brood over her words and the words he had spoken, and to wonder if his words might be true, and if so, how at age eighty-nine he would accomplish what he'd promised. He glanced back up the river again, but Tom's windmill and barn had disappeared.

How might things have been different if he had welcomed Bertram with open arms when he and Sally showed up, he wondered. How might things be different now? Might providence have repaid him today by sending somebody down to check the cows, somebody who might have repaid more kindness in kind? No, that was a silly thought, he knew. Life didn't work that way. No, like all the disappointments and setbacks of his eighty-nine years, he had to somehow work his way around this one.

Reuben was encouraged by the slackening rain. He began to concentrate on the debris that floated around them for some tool he might use, a pole, a board, a scrap of rope, anything that might be of use in either nudging their chicken house toward land, or as an alternative, lashing it to a tree where they could wait out the flood, though how long they could survive without food, and especially without water, he did not know. If only he had something like the one by four oar he'd used to paddle out to Palmer.

Now that the rain was reduced to a light drizzle, visibility was improving. On the other hand, he realized, catching water in his hands was no longer feasible. He should have devoted himself to that enterprise when he had the chance. But now that he could see farther behind and ahead he concentrated on reconstructing his memory of the landscape and landmarks between their farm and Dover. By road it must be about twenty miles. The river ran southeasterly instead of east-west and north-south like the roads, but it also meandered, so the distance by river must be about the same if not greater. If they were moving at a mile an hour or more, that would be perhaps fifteen to twenty hours. If they had begun their river journey somewhere around six in the morning, that would put them at the Highway 81 bridge at—after dark! Then he remembered the old county road bridge, a rickety bridge that was little used, but which, if it hadn't washed out, they would likely reach before dark. But given its disuse, even if it still stood, was it likely that anybody would be there to see them? For now there was nothing to do but ride, watch and think.

Across the Cimarron

CHAPTER 21

It was an exquisite spring morning when Bertram and Sally showed up at the Westerfield claim, mid May of 1893. Three months had passed since Ruth and Reuben had buried little Jacob on the rise west of the house, not far from the spring. Ruth had chosen that spot so she could carry water to the rose bush and lilacs she would plant beside the grave.

But three months is just a blip of time, a second in the eternity it might take to emerge from such grief and loss. Reuben did his best to keep his spirits up, or at least to pretend, and to occupy Ruth's mind with anything he could think of that would keep the tears from her eyes. Occasional visits with the Webers helped, but that was only temporary. There was no mending the hurt that had torn her soul, at least not in a time he was able to foresee. Too often they ate their meager and monotonous meals in silence, and in bed Ruth often wept quietly and would not be comforted, let alone respond to his feeble attempts at love.

Though the date of the awful day was irrelevant from any practical or logical point of view, she seemed unable to put aside the fact that her tiny, gaunt son had breathed his last on February 14, Valentine's Day. She was doubly gripped by the power of this irony, that the day of love brought instead agony and self-loathing, a pain far greater, and certainly more enduring, than the day she brought Jacob into the world.

They had just finished their breakfast of dry flat pancakes, with no butter or molasses and only water to wet their throats. Ruth rose silently and poured a little water into the basin to wash the dishes, and Reuben stepped outside to gather tools for the morning's work of planting beans and corn in the garden. A meadow lark perched atop an apple sapling in the orchard, singing his seven note song. Puffy clouds floated above the river in a brilliant sky. Reuben laid his shovel and hoe aside and went back into the sod house. He circled his arms around Ruth's waist and drew her close. "Leave the dishes for now," he said. "Come out with me to hear the meadow lark."

Without speaking, Ruth laid her wash cloth aside and dried her hands on her apron. She allowed Reuben to guide her to the door and out into the morning sun. He led her to the chopping block where he split firewood and drew her onto his lap. "Listen to the music, darling," he said, holding her on his knees. "It's a perfect spring day, and everything is coming back to life. We have to do that too," he coaxed. "We will try again, just as we must. We'll have another child, but this time you'll be stronger. We'll grow a great crop this year, and by fall we'll have a cow. We'll go into winter with the dugout full of vegetables and butter and cheese. We'll grind our own wheat and have all the bread we can eat. I know it's difficult now," he added, "but please, let's try to go on. We can't forget our tragedy, but let's try to live through it, to be strong enough to work for a future. We still have each other, and we have this good farm and the spring. You'll see. Life will be good again."

"Yes," Ruth replied at last. "We'll try." He held her tight and she laid her head in the hollow of his neck.

For a time neither moved, afraid to break the fragile moment, neither wanting to separate and go to their tasks, to again be alone. It was then that Ruth noticed a wagon cover, and then the heads of a pair of mules just clearing the rise above Salt Creek. "Somebody's coming," she said.

The mules materialized and slowly drew closer, tired old mules it appeared, their sluggish stride challenged by the climb, and behind them a creaking wagon, one of its wheels wobbling as it turned. One occupant of the wagon wore a straw hat, the other a bonnet, both pulled low over their faces. It wasn't until they were quite close that Reuben recognized the man with the reins in his hands. It had been years since they had seen each other, but it had to be Bertram.

"Hello," the driver called, and he waved his hand. Yes, the hand was that of a Negro. Bertram had come.

Ruth slipped off Reuben's knees and the pair stood and watched the wagon pull to a stop. Only then did Reuben break his trance. "Ruth's father tol us where we'd fin you," Bertram called as he slid down from the wagon and helped the woman to the ground, "once we got to Wichita. Oh, this is my wife, Sally."

Now Ruth moved toward the pair. In Wichita she of course had seen Negroes, though she had known none, but she offered the woman her hand. "My name is Ruth," she said.

"And I am Sally Washington," the other woman said, her smile and eyes lighting her face.

"Hello Bertram," Reuben said finally, advancing and taking Bertram's hand. "What brings you here?"

"Same as you I spose," Bertram said. "Hope to get myself a piece of lan. Cain't nobody buy lan in Kansas, less he's got a pocket of gold. We thought maybe you could help us out wit some advice."

"I don't know that I can help you Bertram," Reuben said. "We've got all the trouble we can handle with just ourselves. It's not easy to stay alive here, not even for white folks. And now the free land is gone, unless of course you want to go practically to Texas, where they say it never rains. Not that we get much here either. So I don't know. If I was you, maybe I'd just stay in Kansas, where there's work to be had."

"Thas jus the trouble," Bertram said. "What with the drought and the price of wheat, there ain't much fiel' work. An now with what they call the "panic," banks gone broke, railroads busted, they ain't jobs to be had. Anyhow you know well as I does that a Negro is the las man to get hired for a job in town."

"Yes, I understand that, and I'm sorry for you Bertram, but I just don't know what I could do to help."

"Maybe jus tell us where we might sleep for awhile, whilst we look aroun for somethin to do? I ain't askin you to take us in. I know you cain't do that. But maybe they's a shed on somebody's farm where we could have a roof of some kind, just temporary, til we can get a place of our own."

"And how are you going to do that?" Reuben asked. "Like I said, all the good free land is gone. You'd have to pay cash money, even if you find somebody who's giving it up and going back home, which I hear some have done."

"Well," Bertram drawled, patting his pocket, "we got us a little pot of money, not much, not after gettin this rig and the mules, but if I can jus fin some work, someday we might have enough together to buy a place. In the meantime, these old mules still got a little pull in em, and maybe they's somebody got lan and a plow, but no way to pull it."

"That would be us," Ruth said quietly. "Except we don't have a plow. All we have is land. Nothing to work it with, not even a milk cow, pretty much nothing except what you see." She turned to Reuben. "Maybe they could sleep at least a night or two in the dugout?" she asked. "I could stack our things aside and make a little room."

Reuben cast a look toward Ruth that was not pleased. "But what then?" he asked. "What does that get anybody?"

"That would be very fine of you, Miss Ruth," Bertram said, "but we couldn impose on you. Maybe they's someplace else you could tell us of."

"No, there's no place else," Ruth added, returning Reuben's stare.

"O.K.," Reuben said at last. "For a night or two." Then recognizing that in Ruth's eyes he had appeared unkind, he offered the guests a drink of water.

Ruth brought out a left-over pancake and tore it in two for Bertram and Sally and handed them each a cup of water. The sun was growing warmer, so they leaned against the sod wall on the shady side.

"So, you've seen Father," Reuben said. "And how are the folks?"

"Well, they doin fine, I guess," Bertram replied. "Leas they was when we lef out the end of winter. Gettin older, but still eatin every day, and the old man hasn softened up a bit so far as I can see." Then, as if he felt he'd spoken too disrespectfully, he added, "but at leas they tol us where you ended up an how to fin Ruth's folks in Wichita. Turns out it weren't as easy as it soun. Had to ask people long the way. Nobody seem to know bout you but the man at the Lacey Store."

"Did you—did you tell them about us," Reuben asked, "about father I mean?"

"No, course not," Bertram replied, as if the question was a silly one. "I know well enough how things is, that you don need people knowin that kind of thing out here, specially when you tryin to start a new life. No, that nobody's business but mine, well, an yours."

"What business!" Ruth demanded, the first time in months her voice had raised except perhaps when alone in the house she found herself screaming or demanding reasons why. "That you, Reuben, and Bertram have the same father, that you're— brothers?"

"That's right, Ruth," Reuben said. "It's a long story. I didn't ever see the need or the chance to tell you. But yes, it's true. My daddy had relations with Bertram's mother. She was the daughter of his daddy's slave back in Tennessee. So now you know."

There was an awkward time of silence, then Ruth spoke again. "Well, in that case, of course you can stay in the dugout— as long as you need to. We'll be happy to have you as guests." She stared defiantly into Reuben's eyes.

"Yes, of course she's right," he said at last. "We'll help you if we can, but Lord knows we have little to give."

"We wouldn ask for you to give us nothin," Bertram replied, "cept maybe advice. And I and my mules is ready to help you anyhow we can."

Across the Cimarron

CHAPTER 22

Before dawn the next morning, Bertram Washington set out on foot for Okeene. He thought the mules were too exhausted to trudge another twenty miles round trip. It would be a long walk, but by now the trail was well defined. Reuben walked with him to the west edge of his claim, past the spring and the ten acres of wheat, across the unbroken prairie that was in full bloom with myriad wild flowers—black-eyed susans, coneflowers, wooly verbena, hoary puccoon and many that neither man knew. The wheat was just knee high, dwarfed by insufficient rain, and the heads were small and not well filled, not the fat four-inch heads Reuben had harvested in Kansas. It was too late for rain to help much now, even if it came, though if nothing else happened there would be at least a little wheat to harvest. And yet there was a heart-swelling beauty to the crop, the meager heads bobbing in sea-like waves in the wind. And for the first time in Reuben's life it was his crop.

"It don look too good, do it?" Bertram observed. "Look like a lot of work fo not much grain."

"I'm afraid you're right," Reuben replied. He plucked a head and shelled the grain from the chaff into his hand and chewed the still doughy seeds. The flavor was right, but he knew that once the grains dried hard, they'd be shriveled and small. "I'm glad I have a little seed wheat left, since I'm not sure what kind of crop this seed would produce, even with plenty of rain. But with the dry weather, it's maturing early. I'm guessing it will be ready to harvest in a couple of weeks."

"Well, you can count on me and Sally to help," Bertram offered. "That is, if we still welcome. An if I don fin somebody in town that can point me to a job and a place for us to stay. An don worry. In town I'm just a hired han lookin for a job of work, happenin to be at yo place fo a few days."

"Look, Bertram, I'm sorry about how things are, and about how I acted yesterday," Reuben said. "It shouldn't be this way, but you know how people are. You're good to offer help, and Lord knows we can use all the help we can get."

The brothers parted at the edge of the Westerfield claim. Reuben stood scanning the prairie that stretched to the western horizon until Bertram disappeared behind the ridge. Reuben felt uneasy about the unexpected arrival of his father's other son, but he also couldn't help feeling dirty about not acknowledging Bertram as his brother, especially about keeping the secret from Ruth. But he'd seen how people acted when they knew. That was one of his reasons for leaving Tennessee for Kansas. He knew how people thought in Tennessee, and even in Kansas there were plenty who would take it upon themselves to run a black man out of the territory, and maybe even a white man who took him in. He remembered the black family and the man he now knew as Breedlove waiting that night on the other side of the river. He wasn't sure how his few new neighbors would react if they knew the truth. It wasn't likely that Bertram and Sally would be especially welcome in the neighborhood, and especially not in town. But Bertram had learned how to behave himself, and wasn't likely to stir up trouble. Plus his brother was a strong man and a good worker, and there was going to be plenty of work to do in the next few weeks. Maybe people would overlook the color of his skin, at least for now.

Reuben had heard that a handful of Negroes had settled a few miles down the river, a few during the run, and others who came later and took marginal land that hadn't been claimed. Maybe Bertram and Sally could get a foothold there. But for now he ought to be happy that they had come. He could certainly use a good hand bringing in his meager harvest, and maybe Sally would in some way help divert Ruth's mind from the great sorrow, give her something else to think about, another woman to talk to, even if it was a Negro woman.

Reuben turned from his contemplation and meandered back across the prairie toward home. His legs rustled through green shoots of blue stem, buffalo grass and Indiangrass that was already knee high, native grasses drawing as only they were able to do on deep roots that enabled them to survive the long periods of drought these plains had no doubt seen. That this was dry country was obvious. The only trees were along creeks and the river and in a few wetter valleys and ravines. It remained to be seen whether it was too dry for wheat, fruit trees and the other crops he hoped to grow. Certainly the first year had not been promising.

That realization had gnawed at Reuben for a year now. Thirteen months had passed since the run, and moisture had been far more scarce than he'd anticipated, far less rain than the posters promoting farming on this land had promised. What if this was normal here? Recently he hadn't been able to put that question out of his mind. What if this land wouldn't grow wheat after all? He knew that not long ago great herds of bison had roamed here, and he had found a few bones, a femur, a few ribs and a couple of skulls, but from what he'd heard in Okeene the prairie had been strewn with bones before the cattlemen that leased the Indian land had come. When other ranch work was slow, cowboys had gathered up the bones and shipped them east, where Reuben had been told they brought seven dollars a ton for making fertilizer.

Thinking about the skimpy crop of wheat in his ten planted acres, Reuben wished he had a herd of cows—not just a milk cow, though just the thought of a milk cow brought sadness and shame —but a herd of cows. Maybe that was what this country needed, instead of wheat. But he had no herd of cows, not even one measly milk cow, so he had no real choices to make. They would live or die here by wheat, at least for now.

Though Reuben's legs swished through green grass and myriad prairie flowers, under his feet lay a thick mat of thatch that crunched with every step, dried vegetation that had accumulated in the two summers since the government moved the big ranchers off the Indian land. Amidst the green, heads of dry grasses stood to his waist. This great carpet of dry vegetation had been among his worries all winter long, at least when no snow covered the ground. He'd heard tales of raging prairie fires, and indeed had witnessed a fire west of Wichita that consumed miles of prairie and wheat. He knew that if a fire should ignite during a storm, wind could drive it across the prairie as fast as a man could run, and nothing would stop the inferno until either it reached a river or rain snuffed it out. He had carefully cleared around the dugout, the sod house, the garden and the orchard, and had left a narrow strip unplanted around the wheat field, just in case, but he knew that the ripening wheat was now as vulnerable as the grass to a wind-driven blaze.

When Reuben reached the house, Ruth and Sally were busy canning the first garden beans. In the three months since they had lost Jacob, Ruth had remained listless and quiet, unable to shake off the sorrow that gripped them both. More than once Reuben had found her back in bed after breakfast dishes were done, and while he carried water from spring to garden she might sit on the log by the little stone marker for an hour at a time, weeping silently. He tried everything he knew to bring her back from this dark well of sorrow. He held her in his arms, tried to cheer her with words, played her favorite songs. He insisted that he needed her help with hoeing, carrying water, anything that might take her mind from her awful grief. So his heart was lifted by the sight of the two women at work together, trimming and cutting long green beans, stuffing them into jars, running them through the pressure cooker that whistled on the stove. This woman, this stranger, this Negro woman seemed to have brought some influence that he had not found, some connection that he realized sadly, excluded him. But at the same time he felt a joy and a sense of hope that he hadn't experienced for some time. He knew now that if for no other reason, they had to take Bertram and Sally in, not just because of their need, but because of his need, and of Ruth's even deeper need that he had not been able to fill.

So Reuben withdrew from the door as quickly as he had come, murmured something about how good the beans would be come winter, then immediately excused himself to get back to his watering task before the sun grew hotter. For the first time in many weeks, he realized, he too had seen light filtering through their dismal veil, the dark cloud that had enveloped Ruth and him in lonely isolation. He lifted his eyes to the clear blue sky in thanksgiving, then gathered his buckets and headed for the spring.

Across the Cimarron

CHAPTER 23

Reuben's shoulders ached from carrying pairs of full buckets, one after another, from the vital source that made life in this increasingly parched country possible to long rows of beans, potatoes, onions, corn, tomatoes, squash and greens. Once everything growing in the garden had received its twice-weekly drink, the fruit trees would come next. The saplings they had dug from Ruth's father's orchard in Kansas had survived the crucial first summer and winter, four kinds of apple and two each of cherry, pear and peach. Ten trees, two full buckets each, and the trip from spring to orchard and back nearly a hundred steps each way. He knew that because he had counted them in the monotony of his work. Sometimes it was better to focus mindlessly on the task at hand than to give the mind free range. That or concentrate on a future to imagine and build, anything to keep the mind occupied or dulled to sorrow or fear.

He stood straight to stretch his strained back and gazed across his small field of wheat. There was little green left in stalk or head. With the heat and wind, he calculated it would be ready to harvest within a week. For now there was only water to haul. The late morning sun had grown hot and his shirt was wet with sweat, but the south wind was dry and cooling, and the image of Ruth and Sally at peaceful work buoyed his spirit and allowed his mind to leap ahead and plan. More than it had for a long time, his mind felt free to dream.

Passing half a day in treks from spring to garden and orchard always raised the question of whether there might be a better way of accomplishing the task, some way of transporting water besides at the ends of his arms. They had planted the orchard on just the right slope east of the spring, but the water rose from the earth in a shallow ravine, several feet below the surrounding plain. He was unable to tell whether the spring and the creek bed were actually lower than the garden and the orchard, but that was how it appeared. Digging a ditch to move the water did not seem feasible.

Perhaps they should have planted the trees farther downstream. But that would have put the orchard on a less than ideal slope, and farther from the house. Anyway, too late to worry about that now. Perhaps next spring he would plant the garden in a lower place that he could irrigate by ditch, but the orchard was set. A windmill and a well beside the creek would solve the problem, but that was another thing they couldn't afford anytime soon. So today as he traversed the well-worn path, Reuben's mind worked at possible mechanical devices he might create that would save his back and his time from this perpetual work.

He could, of course, dig a ditch from above the bank so he could carry water up from the spring to the ditch and it would flow down to the trees, but especially in times of drought, when water was needed most, much of the water would be absorbed by dry earth or evaporated into dry air before reaching its destination. If after the work of digging a canal that would shorten the carrying to a quarter of the distance to the orchard, if then only half the water reached the trees, where would be the gain?

What about a homemade windmill of some sort? Would it be possible to construct something of available wood that might lift water ten feet above the spring to the surrounding plain? How about digging a well beside the orchard and drawing up water by rope? So preoccupied by primitive engineering calculations he was that Reuben had long since stopped counting steps or trips from spring to thirsty garden and trees, until he heard Ruth's voice calling that dinner was ready. And only then did he stretch his back straight again and take in the long horizon beyond the narrow world that had occupied him for three hours or more. And only then did he see that above the southern horizon billowed a puffy white cloud. It had to be smoke.

White smoke could mean only one thing, burning vegetation. The prairie must be on fire. Instantly he was gripped by apprehension. He licked his finger and raised it to the wind. Indeed, the wind was from the southwest, the direction of the smoke. He breathed deeply. He couldn't be sure, it could be his imagination, but it seemed he already smelled burning grass.

What to do? There was certainly no fire department to call. He had now met a handful of neighbors to his south and his west, but whether any of them had sensed the danger, he had no idea. In any case, what could a handful of people with shovels and a few buckets of water do? He stooped to the spring and filled both buckets to the brim and strode toward the sod dwelling as fast as he could go without the water splashing out. With two buckets of water he could at least soak burlap bags for fire-fighting tools. He set the buckets by the door and burst into the one-room house. "There's fire coming!" he blurted, then instantly wished he'd stayed more calm. Alarming Ruth and Sally would do no good. So as calmly as he could, he described the cloud in the southwestern sky. "Probably something under control," he said. "Or if not, it will probably miss us. But we ought to be prepared."

Be prepared. Easier said than done. How does one prepare to fight a prairie fire with two buckets to fill at the spring and half a dozen gunny sacks? He rushed to the dugout and pulled a roll of sacks from a corner shelf. He grabbed the shovel, scythe and rake, the only tools he could imagine doing any good, and headed back to the house. Ruth was already at the door with an armful of wetted rags and a jug of drinking water. Ruth and Sally pulled their bonnets tight, and the three of them headed up the hill toward the smoke.

"I smells it," Sally said. "I wonder where Bertram be. I guess he in town by now an won be back soon."

"Well, I guess there are two things we can do," Reuben said. "We can wait here for the fire to come, or we can go to meet it. I guess that's what we'd better do." The three strode toward the now billowing pillar of white, Reuben with full buckets of water sloshing against his legs, the women carrying the gunny sacks, water jug and tools.

"We'd best stop for the Webers," Ruth said. At the ridge they paused for a moment to speculate about how far away the fire was and the speed of the wind. Reuben thought the smoke was perhaps three or four miles distant, but with a stiff wind, gusts of maybe twenty miles an hour, it would travel fast. They altered their course toward the neighbor's house.

Peter Weber had been chopping weeds in the garden when he smelled the smoke and was just rushing to the house. "I'll harness the team," he said, gawking at Sally as if he'd never seen a woman without blond hair and blue eyes. "I'm not sure what good that will do, but maybe we can haul water, or if worse comes to worst, we can all get on the wagon and get away to the river. Come on, Reuben. You can give me a hand."

"Where'd the darky come from?" he asked on the way to the shed.

"Just showed up a day or two ago," Reuben replied. "She and her husband are looking for a place. He's gone to Okeene to see if he can find work or a place to stay."

"You don't mean to say they're staying at your place," Weber said in surprise.

"Yes, just for a little while," Reuben answered, then quickly added, "They're sleeping in the dugout. Actually Sally has been a good help, and her husband seems a decent sort."

Peter looked skeptical. "Well, maybe you should send them down the river," he said. "You've probably heard there's a gaggle of Negroes camped a few miles south."

When the team was harnessed and the wagon ready, the men loaded Peter's tools and they and the women climbed on board. They angled toward Spring Creek to fill Peter's buckets and headed toward the widening column of smoke. The team trotted down the draw, then pulled more slowly on the incline to the next ridge. "Oh my gosh!" Peter hollered from the driver's seat. "I can see the flames. But I'm not sure what we can do. It must be half a mile wide and it's moving fast!"

"Salt Creek might stop the east end," Reuben said. "But there's nothing to stop what's coming our way."

"I wonder if anybody else is fighting it," Peter said. "We may as well get closer and see, and if we have to get away I'm sure the horses can stay ahead." He clucked up the team, which smelled the smoke and balked at moving toward the fire.

"Somebody coming from the west," Reuben said. He cupped his hand over his eyes and squinted for a better look. "Somebody on horseback, coming pretty fast."

The rider apparently spotted the wagon, and altered his course toward them. He leaned into the horse's neck and rode hard, as if to escape the cloud of dust raised by the pounding hooves. As the horseman drew near, Reuben saw that it was a big horse, a reddish brown bay sprinkled with gray. It was the stallion he had seen twice before, the other side of the river before the run, and twenty minutes later when horse and rider materialized just as they now appeared, in a cloud of dust, moving at a full gallop as if to overrun the party that labored up the hill in the wagon. And now they were close enough that Reuben also recognized the man.

The rider pulled the reins only when in another moment the horse would have plowed into the wagon. The steed no more flinched at the close encounter than did the man; apparently it was accustomed to such handling—or feared any deviation from its master's command. The pair came to a stop not ten feet from the wagon.

When the cloud of red dust had passed, the rider's eyes fell on Reuben. "And so," he said, "we meet again."

"And again not under the best of circumstances, I'm afraid," Reuben replied. "But clearly we have a fight on our hands, and I'm glad you've come."

The other man did not break his gaze, and for a moment did not reply. "Well," he said at last, "I haven't forgot that you're the man that took the land I picked. Nor that you threatened to kill me too."

"No, nor have I," Reuben replied. "But I expect you'd have done the same if you'd been in my shoes."

"OK, so we have a fire to fight," Breedlove said, maintaining his searing stare. "But don't forget that I will not forget."

"I understand that," Reuben said. "But now we're neighbors, so maybe we ought to try to start fresh." He stood up from the wagon box and extended his hand. "My name is Reuben

Westerfield," he said. This is my wife Ruth, and these are my neighbors, Peter and Esther Weber."

Breedlove ignored the hand. "And the darkie? Is that another neighbor of yours?"

"This is Sally," Ruth put in. "She's helping me with the canning. She and her husband are looking for work and a place to stay."

"Well, I guess you know my feelings about that," the rider said. "My name is Arden Breedlove. In case you don't know, I live four miles west. Not so nice a place as yours," he added with a sneer thrown Reuben's way. "I guess your spring is still flowin good. The only water I have in this drought is a little seep, just enough to drink and to water the stud and the bull. It must be nice to have a garden too, not to mention a wife and a darkie to tend it."

Reuben dropped his extended hand. "All right," he said, "what can we do to stop this fire?"

"So far as I know, there are no houses in its path up to here," Peter Weber said. "Only prairie and a few patches of wheat. If I don't miss my guess, it's heading pretty much straight for your wheat field, Reuben. If we can spread along the southern and western edges with water and gunny sacks and the tools we have, we might be able to save the wheat, and if we do that, maybe we'll also save your orchard and garden. It's green enough along the creek to stop that flank, and the rest will eventually hit the river, and that should put it to a stop."

"That sounds like a good plan," Reuben said. "And Ruth and I thank you all for your help," he said, looking into Breedlove's scornful face.

Peter turned the horses back toward the Westerfield place, and the ill-equipped team of six spread themselves along the edge of the little wheat field. If they couldn't hold the line, the wheat would burn as readily as the parched prairie grasses. So the crew went to work, Peter and Reuben cutting a swath of prairie grass outside the field with the scythes, the others working with shovels and rakes, clearing the fallen grasses to create a firebreak.

They had cleared a strip three strides wide across the edge of the field, and none too soon. The blaze was so near they could hear the crackle of combustion. They threw the tools on the wagon and spread the buckets of water along the line. They soaked the gunny sacks and worked their way up the firebreak, thrashing the ground with the wet burlap. Now the fire was close enough they could feel the heat. Only moments and they would have to retreat. Either their line would hold, or it wouldn't. They had done all they could do.

"All right, you women run for the wagon," Reuben shouted at Ruth. He threw the bags into his two buckets of water, now almost empty, and backed into the wheat, driven back by the advancing inferno. Peter followed suit, and Arden Breedlove mounted the roan and rode to the west end of the line. Esther drove the team east, beyond the threatening blaze.

In moments the leaping flames hit the break at the eastern edge of the field. The heat they pushed before them immediately dried the grass stubble almost as if it hadn't been wet, but yes— the flames were dying down as the fuel supply was consumed. It looked as if that part of the line might hold. Reuben glanced west. The fire was still fifty yards back from the wheat. Breedlove was off his horse, dragging a clump of burning grass along the front, setting a backfire that was slowly eating toward the oncoming blast, widening the gap between the front and the field.

As soon as the oppressive heat would permit, Reuben and Peter moved back toward the front and began to work the line, thrashing hot spots with the wetted sacks. But then a gust of wind swept over the ridge and lifted a swirl of embers into the air and carried them into the wheat, and instantly the fire revived. Breedlove saw it too, and he was back on his horse. He spurred the stallion toward the new flames, and the three converged around the widening circle of black, beating the new blaze with a fury that they all knew was their last chance. And finally it was contained. A blackened spot fifty feet wide still smoked, but the rest of the wheat was saved.

For the first time the men straightened their backs and wiped the sweat and grime from their faces. They stood in a clot and watched the fire race past the wheat field and across the prairie, a raging front half a mile wide, toward the Cimarron. At least now he would have one less thing to worry about, Reuben realized.

There would be no more prairie fires this year to threaten the things he had planted and built.

"Well, it looks like we did it," he said. "I can't thank you enough Peter, nor you, Arden," he said. Again he extended his hand. Breedlove stared long at Reuben's calloused hand, and finally extended his own. "And now let's join the women and ride over to the house to wash off the soot," Reuben said, "and have some cool spring water and something to eat."

CHAPTER 24

Two years had passed since the prairie fire, three since the run. The drought had not loosened its grip, and what people were now calling a "depression" had only grown worse. Thousands of men roamed the nation looking for work. They even drifted into Cheyenne Arapaho country, hoping to find some back corner of land that nobody had claimed, or perhaps a temporary job of some kind. Arden Breedlove spent as much time in the saloon as he did on his claim, so he saw them all, at least those who happened through Okeene. He had scratched up a few acres and planted a little wheat and oats to feed his animals through the winter, and to satisfy the requirement for proving up on the land. Being from Missouri, he even planted a little corn, but that wilted before the ears could form. Though he devoted little energy to being a farmer, he was able to grow enough grain to feed Boomer, his Hereford bull and the donkey he'd won in a card game with a green settler who'd had a drink too many and fell for Arden's goading into a hand of poker.

Breedlove had never intended to stay on the claim, and still didn't see himself as a permanent homesteader or as part of the community. He dreamed of moving on, and had even thought about going to Mexico as a land speculator, but given the drought and the number of homesteaders who'd given up the fight and moved on, or more likely back where they'd come from, there was no way he could sell his quarter for the kind of money he'd hoped for when he made the run. So after three years, and against all intentions, he found himself settling in.

Before long Arden knew most every homesteader in the country, and they all had heard of him. He was gruff and sometimes rude, but he had what everybody who owned a cow or a mare but no bull or stud needed, so sooner or later most men showed up at his shack, riding or leading an animal to be bred. Now that he had the donkey he could even breed mares to produce mules, which most people preferred for the hard labor of breaking sod and working fields. So Arden came to think of the saloon as a sort of office, a place to meet clients and tell them about the top quality breeding stock he could put to their use.

Arden prided himself on getting by without the back-breaking toil he saw his neighbors exerting. Since the day he'd caught the train out of Fort Scott he'd had nobody else to worry about, and he brought in enough hard cash from his breeding service and card games to buy food and drinks in town. His cabin was in the same sad state or worse than when he'd driven the last nail, but he didn't worry because he had a tin roof that kept out the rain. If he drank too much or if the weather was bad, he even spent a night in the hotel, where he luxuriated in a bath tub as long as the water stayed warm.

It was at the hotel that he met Dawn. She was the daughter of Black Coyote, who lived on the allotment he had chosen by the river. But times were exceptionally lean, and Black Coyote and his wife had younger children to feed and rarely enough to go around. Dawn ventured into Okeene looking for a way to support herself. It happened that the hotel was looking for somebody to clean rooms and wash dishes and to wait on tables when business was good. There was no white woman available to take the job, and Dawn could speak enough English, more than some of the homesteaders, so she was hired. She was eighteen, lean and strong, and in her own way good looking. Whatever resentment of white settlers she shared with her father she was able to hide, and soon most people almost forgot that she was an Indian.

Though he often felt lonely, and especially at night still thought about Maggie and wondered what had become of her, Arden had not entertained the idea of taking another wife. Even if he'd had such thoughts, there was no likely woman to be had; few women had ventured into this raw frontier alone. So one evening as he gnawed at a tough piece of meat he'd scooped from his bowl of soup, his eyes followed Dawn and he began to think that it might be good to take her home.

At first she resisted his advances. After all, he was old enough to be her father, she had seen that he sometimes drank too much, there was an ugly scar across his cheek and he even walked with a limp. On the other hand, he was well-known in the territory, even respected by some, and he seemed to have enough money to spend. Perhaps more important, he had always been polite to her. So one day when she was not working she agreed to ride with him to his homestead and have a look.

He mounted Boomer, pulled her up behind him on the saddle and turned the stallion toward home. They didn't talk on the way; in fact they'd talked very little in the weeks they had come to know each other. But when they reached his house and dismounted, she was dismayed at the squalor in which Arden lived. His abode was an unpainted wooden shack about twelve feet square, with no windows and a loose-fitting door. Inside there was a little stove, a grimy table with two chairs and a sagging bed. The house was considerably smaller and less comfortable than the teepee in which her family spent summers or the small sod house Black Coyote had built for winter.

Arden took her for a walk around the place, past his oat and wheat fields to the little patch of woods around the seep where he drew water, and to the barn. The stable where the three breeding animals lived was actually larger and better built than the house. It was obvious to Arden that she was not impressed, and seeing the place through her eyes rather than his own, eyes that had grown blind to crudeness and even filth, he understood that he could not win her, or any other woman, without making changes.

He had not prepared to do so, but he found himself asking Dawn to be his wife. He promised that he would have a bigger and better house built, with the cleanliness and all the conveniences that a home in such a place could provide, and that he would wait for her answer until the house was done. She was non-committal, but agreed she would consider the offer when the house was built.

So suddenly Arden was in need of a carpenter. His experience —besides playing cards and choosing breeding stock—consisted of farming skills that better fit rocky and wetter Missouri than Oklahoma Territory, laying railroad ties and serving as an officer of the law. He had never built a real house, and had no idea how to begin. He would need to find somebody with skill.

He thought of Peter Weber, whose house he thought might serve as a model and which he thought might satisfy his intended bride. He paid the Webers a visit. They showed him the house, and Peter described the materials used and the construction processes, but said that he himself was about to embark on a larger building project, a barn for hay and for the few cattle he had acquired. He recommended Reuben Westerfield as the best carpenter around.

This presented a dilemma for Arden Breedlove. He did not relish the idea of even visiting Westerfield, let alone asking him for help. He was pretty sure it would be unpleasant to work with the man who'd stolen the place he'd intended to claim. He decided to check around town for another carpenter. He found men who wanted work, but nobody who had ever built a house. Even if he'd found somebody else with the necessary tools and skills, most of the homesteaders had their hands completely full trying to wring a meager existence from their land. Summer was winding down, and if he hoped to have a house completed in time to bring Dawn there by winter, he had to start soon. Finally he made up his mind to pay a visit to the man he least wanted to see.

Reuben and Ruth were having dinner when he arrived. They invited him in and Ruth insisted on putting on a plate for Arden. Reuben produced a fruit crate for another chair. Now Arden felt doubly beholden to a man he was determined not to like. But he swallowed his pride along with the turnips and beans, and eventually raised the topic of his mission.

Reuben of course had serious qualms about working for Breedlove, but after all, the other man had helped him save his fruit trees and his wheat, and there was no question that he and Ruth needed money. So he promised that once Arden had building materials, he would walk over each day and help build the house for a dollar a day, plus breeding service for two years for the cow he hoped to buy. In his mind he calculated that the house Arden described might take about four weeks to build, so that might add up to twenty-five dollars in his pocket, money for which he could imagine several pressing uses. Arden turned Boomer toward Lacey, where he could order lumber.

Across the Cimarron

CHAPTER 25

Just when Reuben thought the sky might be lightening, the rain resumed. The brief intermission had brought no break in the clouds, but they had thinned enough that the sun's position in the sky was apparent. It was mid afternoon. But now the sky darkened again, and without warning the rain began to pound. The west bank that Reuben had so hoped to reach nearly disappeared.

Suddenly Reuben found himself boiling with rage. He raised his fist and swore at the heavens. "How much more do you expect us to take!" his hoarse voice demanded. "What do you want of us? How much more can we endure? Damn this rain! Damn this raging river! Why did I ever come to this God-forsaken country? A lifetime of work and doing without and struggle after struggle, and this is how it ends?"

As sudden as his wrath was his shame. He had been trying to stay strong and not only convince Ruth that they would get off the swollen river alive, but actually do it, and now he'd broken down like a weakling fool. "I didn't mean that," he confessed to Ruth. "This is not how it ends. We will get off this river alive, and we will rebuild and go on with life."

Ruth did not reply. He didn't know whether she was shocked to silence by his outburst, simply resigned to a fate she foresaw, or too tired and weak to care. But now that rain was falling again, he cupped his hands, collected a few drops and put his hands to her lips, then did the same to ease his own parched throat.

He couldn't escape the irony of facing possible death by flood, and yet parched by thirst. But that was the way things were on these western plains. There was never the right amount of water, it seemed, and rarely at the right time. There had been other floods, not like this, but flood years when crops washed out or rotted from too much rain. Such a year might be followed by one in which seeds would sprout, only to wither and die, or even a few years when seeds lay dormant in the fields without enough moisture to germinate.

The fifties were bad enough, but the thirties were the worst, of course. But at least by the thirties they had a good well between the new house and the barn and a system of pipes and ditches that would make the garden produce even when no rain fell. They had plenty of chickens and cows and pigs for eggs and milk and meat, and some to sell or trade for things they needed but could not grow. They even had a little money in the bank. So bad as the thirties were, they were nothing like those early years, the years when they needed the most and had the least, years when drought and grasshoppers and the worst depression the country had yet seen made every year appear as if it could be their last on the claim.

What came to be known as the Panic of 1893 turned into an economic depression that gripped the country for the next four years. And the drought they suffered their first year on the homestead they came to see as normal by the time it finally broke in the fall of 1896. So those were the hardest years in almost every way. Yet when the last nail was driven in Arden Breedlove's house in October of ninety-five, Reuben had twenty-six dollars and fifty cents in the jar behind the stove. Funny how the neighbor he'd threatened to kill had pretty much saved them from starving out. Of course much of the money Reuben had earned had come from other men as desperate as himself, he knew, men not wise enough to ignore Breedlove's offer of a game of cards. But he couldn't dwell on that. His responsibility had been to Ruth and to this quarter of land, and later to their second son, John, born in July of 1896, just before the rains returned.

In four summers they had not produced a decent crop of wheat, and what they did raise sold for such a low price that half the proceeds went to the railroad for shipping it out. But at least by their fifth summer on the claim, the summer before he could finally prove up and gain title to the homestead they had dearly earned, they had a milk cow. He'd dug a deep ditch through the creek bank to move water to a system of ditches that would irrigate the fruit trees and the garden, and they were enjoying their first harvests of peaches, apples, cherries and pears. They had a snug log house with a sheet iron roof above their heads. He had traded the Colt pistol for a double-barreled shotgun, so he could take quail and prairie chickens, and in winter when meat would keep without refrigeration, a deer. Six dollars of their savings they would spend the coming April, when he could make the final Homestead Act payment and receive a clear patent to the land, bearing the signature of the newly-elected president, William McKinley. That would leave twenty dollars, the most comfortable margin of their married life. They were closer than they'd ever been to buying a team and wagon and implements so he wouldn't be dependent on trading work and food to borrow from the Webers, but still far short of the dream of building a better house.

They still clung to the margins of security, but they no longer feared immediate disaster—rain pouring through the roof, attacks from hostile Indians or an infuriated neighbor, starvation or the necessity to give it all up and go back to Kansas for a life beholden to the choices of others, an especially bad prospect when thousands of unemployed men trudged the streets of every city vying for the few jobs that could be had. Now the one fear they could not hide from was the fear that they might lose another child.

Thankfully John's birth came easy, on a calm and cool evening in late July. Esther Weber, who now had a son of her own, was there to comfort and help. The baby was plump and healthy, the offspring of a woman well fed with all the meat, milk, vegetables and fruit she needed or wanted. He went quickly to Ruth's breast, which nourished him well. Though neither Ruth nor Reuben could completely put away long-nagging memories and fears, there was no rational reason for this baby not to thrive. And thrive he did. John would prove to be their only surviving child, but he was their great comfort and hope, the son Reuben hoped might carry on their family line.

156

CHAPTER 26

There was, of course, the other family, the family that Reuben had been loathe to acknowledge. What they all expected would be Bertram and Sally's short stay in the Westerfields' dugout lasted through the summer of 1893. Reuben saw how much happier and more spirited Ruth was with Sally's companionship, and Bertram pulled his weight in every task that required another pair of hands. Reuben made it clear from the first that they had no money to pay a hired hand, but Sally and Bertram had no other place to go, and they were content to work alongside their hosts for a share of the abundant food the garden produced and a place to sleep, primitive though that was.

Bertram had made the rounds in Okeene the day of the prairie fire, and several farmers said they'd call on him if they needed help. Of course there was no way to communicate that need except by walking or riding a horse, but a couple of times a neighbor came by and hauled Bertram to their homestead for a few days' work, putting up a building, making hay or building fence. Though Bertram was in Okeene looking for work the day Reuben needed him most, to help fight the fire, he was there every other time Reuben needed help, including the hard work of cutting wheat by hand, shocking it, hauling it in and threshing the grain. By summer's end Reuben had come to depend upon Bertram, even if he did not acknowledge him as his brother.

In September it was clear to all that the garden was playing out and food would be in short supply. The only big task of winter would be cutting and transporting firewood, and Reuben didn't need help with that beyond the use of a wagon and team. In the meanwhile, Bertram had learned about the small community of

Negroes who had staked claims on marginal land to the south, and one day he set out on foot to see what he could learn. Among those he found was Wadron Drake and his wife and kids, the family they would eventually figure out were the ones camped next to Reuben the night before the run. The Drakes had settled on a hilly piece of land three or four miles south of the Westerfields, land that everybody with a horse or a wagon and team had bypassed the day of the run.

Like Reuben, they had dug a burrow into the hillside and built up low walls with sod, then covered the roof with the same tarpaulin they had camped under on the Cimarron. The Drakes welcomed Bertram and told him about the community of black folk, a handful of scattered families who had already come together and established a church that met in the largest of their homes. One of the families had a son who was twenty-one, old enough to claim his own quarter, but who had decided to go back to Arkansas and rejoin a fiancée who did not want to live as a pioneer. Thus, he had never filed a claim on his chosen land.

Wadron and Bertram walked the perimeters of the abandoned quarter. It was mostly hilly, high and dry. The prairie grasses were short, so at least in dry summers like this one it did not appear the most productive soil. Yet with one hundred sixty acres—an unimaginable spread for a man whose parents were owned as slaves and who himself had starved out as a sharecropper on forty acres of farmed out cotton land in Arkansas—the quarter represented the fulfillment of a dream Bertram had never expected to realize. He agreed to pay the young man ten dollars and take over the claim. Bertram would file under his own name, and would send the money as he could. He couldn't wait to get back and tell Sally the good news.

Sally was ecstatic. She insisted that they set out immediately after breakfast next day to see the place. Ruth offered to tag along, and Reuben said he would go as well. Ruth packed a lunch, and by mid morning the four were standing on a hilltop surveying the Washingtons' new estate. They walked the hills until Bertram and Sally settled on a south-facing depression that could be widened in the usual fashion, the removed earth stacked along the edges to raise low walls. The place was half a mile from the river, but Bertram figured his worn-out team could haul cottonwoods from the bottom to construct a roof and door. The tattered tarp would have to serve for now as a roof.

Two years passed, the Westerfields and the Washingtons seeing each other on rare occasions. But then one fall day in 1895 Bertram and Sally showed up at the Westerfield door. Ruth saw immediately that Sally was going to have a baby. They embraced and Ruth invited them in. She stepped back out to call Reuben, who was fitting a log on the back side of the new cabin he was building. He came in, seemingly genuinely happy to see his brother, and certainly to learn their good news. Then Ruth shared her own news. She was pregnant too. Sally's baby was expected in the middle of winter, Ruth's in summer. Remembering her own sad winter birth, Ruth insisted that when the time drew near she be notified so she could be on hand to help.

And so the two families grew closer, drawn not only by the unusual brother bond, but now by common motherhood. Not that they visited regularly. After all, they were separated by four miles of hills with no road between them. But they did stay in touch, getting together now and then for a meal, usually followed by music from Reuben's fiddle or guitar.

When their sons John and Tom were five, the couples and other neighbors began to talk about building a school. The Webers had two children as well, a boy older than Tom and a girl who was three. There were nine other children of school age or nearing that mark in a five mile stretch of river, so they gathered the families together in the Webers' house, still the finest in the neighborhood.

Peter Weber offered to donate an acre on his southwest corner for a school. Peter had inquired of the county superintendent in Kingfisher and was told they might be able to hire a teacher for forty dollars a month. That seemed like a lot of money, and a few families, including the Washingtons, weren't sure they could scrape together their share. But by now most settlers had accumulated meager savings, and every couple agreed that if possible they would put up four dollars per child each month to pay a teacher. The men would get together in early spring before field work to build a one-room log schoolhouse.

They gathered on a sunny day in late February to begin. They drove two teams and wagons to the river bottom, felled a dozen middle-sized cottonwood trees, stripped them of limbs and bark, loaded them on the wagons and hauled them up the Salt Creek valley to the bluff. The next day they shaped and fitted the logs, each trunk making a side log and an end log. They returned each day for a week until the structure was complete, including a roof of rustic shingles Reuben hewed from cedar logs. By fall they would need to find and install a stove and build tables or desks, but otherwise the building was ready. Now to find a teacher and books.

As it turned out, a family living toward Okeene had a sixteen-year-old daughter who had finished primary school and gone off to the new county seat of Watonga for the six week teacher course and had been certified. Myrtle Thompson agreed to teach the dozen pupils for forty dollars a month plus room and board, a responsibility that would rotate from month to month amongst the families. The county superintendent supplied a few used books and a chalk board, and they were in business. However, when the superintendent learned that two of the families were Negroes, he informed them that the Oklahoma Territorial Legislature, citing a five-year-old US Supreme Court ruling, had passed a law requiring the segregation of white and colored students in the territory's schools.

This made little sense to the group of neighbors who had worked together to build the schoolhouse. Whatever their backgrounds and personal feelings might have been, they had coexisted in a generally friendly way. They met again in July, and agreed unanimously to ignore the rule. After all, the territorial capital of Guthrie was a good sixty miles away, and it wasn't likely that anybody that far away would notice or care that people in Forest Township had agreed to defy what they saw as a silly law.

So September came and school began. All went well for the fall term. When the community gathered in the twelve by sixteen schoolhouse for the Christmas program and recitation, it was standing room only for the adults huddled just inside the door. The pupils performed admirably, demonstrating that they had learned the alphabet and could read a few words and that they could add two plus two to equal four and even beyond. But in January Myrtle arrived before the sun was up one morning to build the fire, only to find a crudely lettered note tacked to the schoolhouse door. "No nigers mixing with whites," it read. "Thro them out or the skool will get burnt."

Myrtle was shocked and afraid. She tore the note down and hid it in her apron pocket. She did her best to conduct classes as usual that day, but as soon as the students were dismissed she rushed home with the Weber kids, with whom she was residing that month, and showed the note to Esther. When Peter came in from doing chores Esther shared it with him, and they decided to call a community meeting at the school for the next night. They prepared a note that Myrtle could send home next day with the kids.

The Washingtons and the Drakes of course knew that the threat was directed at them and their children. Fearing that their children would be harmed, or that the school would be burned because of them, both couples offered to withdraw their children from the school. Ruth would not hear of that. "No," she insisted. "We've built the school together for all of our children. We've pooled our money to hire Myrtle to teach them. We cannot allow either some prejudiced neighbor or some politicians to tell us how we'll run our school."

Esther Weber agreed. "We can't watch the school all night to be sure nobody burns it," she said, "but surely we can have the men take turns watching over the teacher and kids while they're at school. We can't let bullies stop us from educating all our children."

There was general assent to what the women had said. And so they agreed that school would go on without interruption, and that the fathers would take turns keeping an eye on the school to be sure nobody was harmed.

But that was not the end. In April they received a letter from the county superintendent with a copy of the territorial law. The superintendent made it clear that their "illegal" school had come to the attention of territorial authorities, and that white and Negro children had to be segregated by the fall term. The two black families thanked their neighbors for sticking together with them, but announced that their children would not return to school in September. They had all learned to read a bit, and they would help them as much as they could at home. The letter mentioned the Plessy v. Ferguson ruling, which said that racial segregation was justified, since "separate but equal" gave everybody the same chance. But how did that have anything to do with them? They had only one school and one teacher, so no sort of "equality" was possible. They all knew the whole situation was absurd, but there was nothing they could do to change the law. So in September school resumed, the white children aware of the void the exclusion of their former classmates had left.

In the momentous year of 1907, the year that John turned eleven and began his sixth year of school, Oklahoma became a state. The territorial legislature was dissolved, and the new state legislature met for the first time in the capital of Guthrie. The first law enacted by the Oklahoma State Senate, Senate Bill 1, enshrined racial segregation into state law. And so it remained for nearly fifty years.

CHAPTER 27

The rain tapered off to a light drizzle, and though the sky was still heavy with clouds Reuben could now see at least a mile of river ahead and behind. They had long since passed the hills where his brother had homesteaded and the valley where his brother's son still lived, but Reuben could not leave behind the memory of injustice. Years later when Tom worked with Reuben in the blacksmith shop he saw how smart Tom was, yet he could barely read simple instructions. Yes, he had taught Tom to play the fiddle for free instead of charging fifty cents a lesson as he had others, but that did nothing to assuage his guilt. He had hardly protested in the face of gross injustice, when he and his neighbors should have stood together and fought. If Reuben had lacked reasons for regret, this memory alone would have been enough.

The brightest spot in the dismal sky was now low in the west. It was hard to judge the time, but it must be late afternoon. They had been on the river for at least twelve hours, with nothing to eat or even to drink since supper the previous day besides the few drops of rain he'd collected in his hands. Their clothing was still damp, but the afternoon had warmed enough that Reuben no longer felt chilled. They were no closer to land than they had been, and in this flatter region there was even less variation in the view—muddy water and in the distance a low strip of earth below a leaden sky. He sprawled across the mossy roof, scanning the long view down river ahead, the monotony broken only by floating debris, and here and there by a treetop protruding from the flood. Then he saw it—a structure jutting from the watery plain, perhaps half a mile away. The county bridge!

He shook Ruth's arm to stir her from dazed sleep. "The bridge is coming!" he said. "Surely there will be somebody there to help us. Now we're going to be OK." He narrowed his eyes to better focus on the structure. He had been across it many times in the old days, the oldest bridge across the Cimarron. It had survived every flood, a tall steel structure with a rickety wooden plank deck that rattled and shook when you crossed by truck or car. It had seen mostly local use after the modern Highway 81 bridge had been built three miles farther downstream, but it had survived for many decades, and so far as Reuben could now determine, seemed completely intact. Surely they would get off the river there.

Now that rescue seemed likely, the progress of their raft across the last expanse seemed painfully slow, the silence broken only by water lapping against the walls. Gradually the rusty girders assumed sharper definition against the gray. When they were close enough, Reuben began to scan the deck for people or cars. He detected no movement. And then he saw why. The current they rode was disrupted by this obstacle. The channel was split in two, diverted around both ends of the bridge. A wide expanse of water covered the approaches, both north and the south. The bridge still stood, but it was an island in a muddy sea.

Now the chicken house reached the point where the two channels began to part. Rudderless, their vessel chose the southern flow. Yet it seemed likely that rather than being swept around the end they still might hit the bridge. It was urgent to form a plan. There was light between the river and the deck, but how much? At first it appeared there was barely room for them and their raft to float under, but as they came ever closer he saw that the water was perhaps four feet below the bridge. "Yes, we can make it out!" he told Ruth. "All we have to do is stand and grasp a truss. I'll pull myself up and then I'll pull you up after. All you'll need to do is hang on for a minute while I climb up." He shook her again, trying to stir her into action. Her arms seemed almost limp. "Let's get up on our knees now," he shouted, tugging at her arms. Painfully slow as their approach to the bridge had seemed, now the distance was closing fast. There would be little time to act.

The bridge was now a stone's throw away. Reuben struggled to his feet and crouched on the bobbing slope. The aged cedar shingles were slick with moss and rain, but Reuben dug his heel into the rotting wood, and tugged at Ruth's arms to raise her up to her knees, and then to her feet. Now the bridge was twenty yards away and they stood almost erect. "We're in luck," Reuben shouted. "We're going to hit the bridge between uprights. Remember, just grab a truss and hang on. I'll have us out in no time."

Ruth did not speak. Her eyes were glazed, her body slack. He hoped she could stand alone once he turned her loose to grab the bridge, now just twenty feet ahead. He turned her so she would hit the bridge straight on and raised her arms. They would hit the deck about Ruth's chest. And now they were there and Ruth's feeble hands were on the iron. "Hang on!" he yelled, scrambling to pull himself up.

He had not anticipated how difficult it would be, his muscles cramped from inaction, his body weak from hunger. But at last he swung a leg over the edge and pulled himself onto the deck. He turned to grab Ruth, but she was gone. She had lost her grip, had slumped back to the roof and was floating on under the bridge. He rushed to the other side, where the chicken house was just emerging. Ruth lay crumpled on her back on the shingles, her eyes now wild with terror. There was only one thing he could do. He lowered himself from the planks on the downriver side and dropped back to the roof. His overshoes slipped on the wet shingles and he slid toward the water. His fingers dug into the rotting wood and stopped his slide just at the edge of the roof. With what seemed his last breath he dragged himself back up the slope to where Ruth lay.

"I'm sorry," she said. "I just couldn't hold on."

Reuben did not answer. He lay gasping for breath, unable to speak. Anyway there was nothing to say. This might have been their best chance, maybe their only chance to get off the river, and they had failed. He massaged his aching knee, which he must have twisted in the fall, his mind working to accommodate itself to the new reality. Not only had they failed, and not only was he fully aware of how weak Ruth had become, but he now questioned whether, given another opportunity to escape, he himself would have the strength. Yet if they were going to get off the river, it was up to him to figure a way. "It's OK," he said at last. "The Highway 81 bridge is just a few miles down the river. We'll find a way to get out there."

And so they floated on, Ruth slipping back into dazed silence, Reuben struggling to stay alert, trying to put the failure behind him, seeking blindly for some new plan for the bridge that lay ahead.

CHAPTER 28

Hadn't it always been like that? Struggling to stay alert. Putting the most recent failure behind. Seeking, usually much too blindly, for a plan for the bridge to come? For most of his eighty-nine years the next step had rarely been clear. Yes, they had survived those early years of drought, and after that more years of deprivation, the loss of their first child, conflict after conflict, decades of twelve-hour days with rarely a true day of rest.

Even after the grueling first fifteen years, when they at last had built a comfortable new home, after their second son had grown into a promising and hardworking young lad, after Reuben had put his hand to everything he knew how to do, used every tool he had from his bare hands to his carpenter hammer, his blacksmith hammer, his fiddle and his guitar, life had not been easy. And then just when John had reached manhood and was setting out to build a life of his own, along came the Great War and took him away.

He wasn't sure Ruth would survive the two long years that John was gone. Driven sick by worry, never able to bury her sorrow over losing Jacob and her inability to have another child after John, she lived in constant fear that John would not come home from war. And then there was Joseph, John and Prairie Star's only child, lost in his prime. Maybe it was all the losses that for a time had made looking forward easier than looking back.

In fact, looking forward had always been the only way he knew to keep moving. Looking ahead was all that had kept them going through the thirties, when year after year crops failed, when he had to shoot the hogs, when many a neighbor lost their farm and had to move on. So every year he convinced himself that next year it would rain, that prices would be better, that when Joe came of age there would be a farm for him. And then, in 1938 when rains finally came, Joe had to ride that damned horse that everybody knew could never be really broken, the descendent of Arden Breedlove's roan.

In the thirties, when there was no work to be had and not much to sell, he had found other ways to bring in a few dollars, hauling fruit to Enid to sell, hiring himself and his team out to the county to maintain roads at two dollars a day, a dollar for him and another for the team, playing at dances every chance he got—until too many neighbors lost their farms and left the country and those who were left seemed to lose even the ambition to gather for relief on a Saturday night.

And yet, in the middle of the Depression and drought, when looking forward was hardest to do, there was the Saturday afternoon when he and Ruth looked back. It must have been 1936 or '37, because they were driving the Chevrolet he'd bought from Jack Bailey, partly because their Model A was shot, but mostly because Jack and his family had lost everything else and needed cash just to move on.

Over the past couple of summers, when his meager wheat crop was out and the ground lay hard and dry, he'd heard more than once on the radio that rain had fallen not far to the southeast, the area where he'd lost his first claim in 1889. The weather bureau had now kept records for four decades, so it was documented that the region south of Crescent received about four inches more rain in the average year than his land west of the Cimarron. Even more important, it was good river bottom land that was sub-irrigated by a shallow aquifer, so crops and pastures and orchards might thrive even in dry years. Like the ancient land between the Tigris and the Euphrates he'd read about, it was a fertile crescent.

The visit was nothing he'd planned. It was a beautiful morning in July, the chores were finished, and there was nothing pressing to do. Looking out across the fields at the sun-baked pasture and the barren soil he'd plowed after harvesting the meager crop of wheat, his thoughts turned as they often did to the river bottom land he had chosen in the run of eighty-nine. He could still see it in his mind, the grove of mature cottonwoods and oaks on the southern slope toward the river, the tall native grasses that sprung from soil rich enough he knew it would grow any seed he planted, the incline just right to hold rain but not flat enough for water to stand, and then of course the river, with abundant water for livestock, the potential for irrigation, and the aquifer where one could get good water from a shallow well.

So at lunch he asked Ruth if she would like to take a ride. She eagerly agreed, also happy to get away from ever present reminders of struggle. "Where are we going?" she asked.

"Just a little ride into what might have been," Reuben answered. "You'll see when we get there." So when the dishes were done they set out to the southeast, across the Cimarron on the new bridge, across the sand hills and the sandy farms to Hennessey, south through Dover to the river again, east to Crescent, south again toward the Cimarron, toward a place the map called Indian Springs. Nothing, of course, looked familiar. How could it, Reuben realized. To have expected to recognize landmarks would have been nothing short of foolish. Nearly half a century had passed, and the land was completely altered by two generations of settler occupation. Already many of the houses appeared old, some perhaps abandoned. There was a dirt road every mile. Most of the trees that would have grown here five decades ago would likely be dead, and around many farm houses stood a grove of young trees, mostly elms.

Besides all that, he wasn't quite sure where he had been the night of April 22, 1889. He drove around a couple of sections, thinking he might have spotted something familiar, but he couldn't be sure. And then off the road to the south he saw a grove of tall trees. The way they rose above the surrounding plain indicated that they must stand on higher ground. He found a driveway and followed that a quarter mile to the trees. On the south edge of the grove stood a barn, a few other outbuildings and a modest frame house, facing the river with a clear view across green alfalfa and pasture land.

Reuben stopped the car and gazed toward the Cimarron. Then he realized he was holding his breath and let it go. He opened the door and got out. The house was well kept and newly painted, white with trim that matched the towering trees. Ruth followed and they walked to the door and knocked. There was no response. Apparently nobody was home. In a way that was a relief. He realized that even though he'd been haunted by thoughts of this place for most of his adult life, one reason he'd never returned was that he feared what he might find, feared that he would knock on the door and it would be answered by the man who had stood over him with a shotgun aimed at his eyes. Or if not that man, then perhaps the claim jumper's son. What would he have said? What could he say?

Reuben and Ruth turned and looked again toward the river. The small creek that Reuben had seen so many times in his mind's eye still snaked from the grove past the farmstead and on south to the river. The bottom land was green with alfalfa. In the grassland to the east fat cattle grazed. Yes, this region averaged more precipitation than they received on the high red plain, but Reuben knew that the difference between his farm and this one could not be attributed to rainfall alone. Clearly the roots of alfalfa and native grasses here reached subterranean moisture in a high water table that underlay the river bottom land. He took Ruth's elbow and guided her toward the creek, then followed that down the quarter mile to the Cimarron.

Neither spoke as they walked. When they reached the water they gazed out across the lazy river, now mostly sandbars and isolated pools. Just as it was at their place forty or fifty miles up the river, here the sometimes wild Cimarron was shrunken to a shallow meandering stream. Reuben turned back north toward the cottonwoods and oaks, the little house and the much larger barn nestled in their arms. The trees were considerably taller than in his memory, but otherwise the scene was much as he had imagined it that day in 1889—and as he had seen it in both waking and sleeping dreams. He realized that his vision had blurred. His eyes were filled with tears.

He wiped a sleeve across his face. "Well, I guess we might as well be heading home," he said. "There will be chores to do." He strode north toward the waiting car, Ruth trailing behind. They bumped out the driveway and did not look back. Reuben rolled down the windows, and the dry summer wind rushed through the car as he drove, the hot dry wind that only drought can bring.

Across the Cimarron

CHAPTER 29

One thing was clear. Nothing was simple. The place they'd called home for fifty years had been a beautiful and quiet refuge, until last night. The house had grown old like them, but it was still a comfortable home. It had been the most modern house in the neighborhood when he'd built it in 1907. He had rigged a pitcher pump to bring water from the cistern and the well through pipes, right to the sink. No more carrying in buckets of water or drinking from a dipper gourd. Life was generally still rather primitive, and even though President Roosevelt had participated in a hunt that killed eleven wolves just two years earlier, wildness had not yet been subdued. But to Reuben that was no reason that his family should not enjoy modern comforts.

The trees amidst which they had built had also grown old, not unlike the cottonwoods of the long-lost claim. It was the oldest and tallest tree, of course, that had attracted the lightning, split down the middle and crashed through the roof. The tree was already mature when they built, and now was perhaps a century old, its girth greater than he and Ruth together could reach around. But he and Ruth and John were not the first to live in its shade.

Broken Lance was already dead when Reuben bought the land in 1906. And it was not Reuben, but a money lender who had separated the aging man from his allotment two years earlier. The fact that Reuben was not directly responsible had always to some degree assuaged the unease he felt when he thought about Broken Lance, but there were times when he awoke in the night from some dream that brought him face to face with the long-dead Indian, and he had long since faced the fact that he had profited from the other man's demise.

It was true, as Breedlove had said that night as they waited on the other side of the river, that the Arapahos "weren't even from here." Why worry about taking somebody else's land if it wasn't really their home? In any case, from what Reuben had heard, they had been somewhat nomadic peoples, not the kind to settle down and work a single piece of land.

But that did not change certain facts. It wasn't that Reuben had gone looking to learn their history. It was more that the history was forced upon him. Black Coyote saw to that. There was that first encounter in the fall of ninety-two when Black Coyote, or Watongah as he called himself, shot the deer at Reuben's spring. They had seen each other occasionally over the years, and though he was not unfriendly, Watongah never failed to make Reuben uncomfortable with his scraps of history. The time came when Reuben could not ignore what he'd been told. He was not a man to deny truth, and he came to understand that the stories Black Coyote told him were true.

The Arapahos had shared a vast region of Colorado with the Cheyenne, a region rich in buffalo and other game. When gold was discovered in Colorado in 1858, prospectors and other wealth seekers poured in. Three short years later the Indian leaders were forced to sign the Treaty of Fort Wise, giving up most of their land. The government demanded that the Cheyennes and Arapahos surrender and gather at the Army fort. With the animals upon which they depended for survival nearly wiped out, the Indians had little choice. So in 1864 the Arapahos led by Chief Left Hand and the Cheyennes led by Black Kettle set up camp near Fort Lyon on Sand Creek.

On November 29 the peaceful camp was attacked by the Third Colorado Regiment under the command of Colonel John Chivington. In what came to be known as the Sand Creek Massacre, soldiers killed and mutilated more than two hundred men, women and children. With no other good options, in 1867 the surviving Southern Arapaho and Southern Cheyenne signed another treaty, the Treaty of Medicine Lodge. They agreed to move to a reservation west of the Cimarron River in Indian Territory, what would later become western Oklahoma.

Twenty years passed, years in which this new reservation land would be leased to cattle ranchers for pennies an acre. And then came the Dawes Act, or the General Allotment Act of 1887. Though their land had already been forcibly whittled away three times in thirty-six years, now each Cheyenne and Arapaho head of household would be "given" one hundred sixty acres to farm. The rest would be opened for free settlement by others, including the Westerfields.

But that was not the end. In 1902 Congress altered the Dawes Act, permitting adult heirs to allotted Indian land to sell the land. By then the tribal cultures were devastated, their population cut in half by dislocation, malnutrition and disease. The Cheyenne and Arapaho, after all, were not farmers. They had no cattle, nor the tools, traditions or desire to farm.

By then bootleggers, loan sharks and exploiters of every stripe were working the territory. Just as they were not accustomed to farming, to the natives alcohol was also foreign. George Bent, an interpreter and trader at the Indian agency in Darlington, plied Indians with alcohol and sometimes ended up with title to their allotted land. Other whites sold things to Indians on credit or loaned them money at usurious rates with their land as collateral. Reuben heard about one banker who loaned Indians money at three hundred and fifty percent interest. Most were illiterate, of course, and could not read what they were asked to sign. In two years, thousands of acres of allotted land were transferred to whites. The land upon which Reuben had built his valley home was such land. It had been the allotment chosen by Broken Lance, Black Coyote's father.

Broken Lance's wife, Makes Her Blanket, had fallen ill. A medicine man at Cantonment had performed a ceremony for her healing, and had given her certain herbs that had been effective in the past, but she continued to fail. Broken Lance thought it was mostly the trauma they had experienced, but whatever the cause, nothing seemed to help. At last he borrowed money from the bank in Okeene. He paid a neighbor to take them by wagon to the train, and they rode the train to see a doctor in Enid. The doctor said Makes Her Blanket needed an operation. There was a tumor on her intestine. She did not survive the surgery. Broken Lance had to buy a coffin in order to bring her body home on the train for burial. Once she was laid to rest, he borrowed more money to pay the doctor bills and the hospital. He had no way to repay what he had borrowed, so at the end of the year the banker foreclosed. Broken Lance went to live out his days with Black Coyote, and the banker put his land up for sale.

Reuben was able to buy the land because after rains returned in 1897, crops were better across the region. By then he had broken nearly half his claim for wheat, so at last some money was coming in. Broken Lance's allotment lay adjacent to his claim, just up the river, so he went to see the banker about the land. He also visited Black Coyote, who was still mourning his father's death. Black Coyote's bitterness had not dissolved, but nevertheless he did ease Reuben's mind. "I'd rather you have it than the banker or some stranger," he said. "You will take good care of my father's land."

Sometimes it seemed to Reuben that spirits haunted the place. He'd long ago carried the skull he'd found amongst the rocks that first day to a secret place beside the creek and buried it by the spring, the spring from which he had drunk that night so long ago, and from which he guessed the person whose eyes had peered from the skull had also drunk. And yet it still sometimes seemed that he heard voices in the rustle of cottonwood leaves. His was not a superstitious mind, but neither could he ignore what he had long ago come to accept. The best parts of the life he and Ruth knew were built in part on the injustice dealt to other human beings. "Perhaps the whole region is tainted by money and blood," he once said to Ruth. "There is little we can do to change the past, but we must acknowledge our debt and repay it as we can."

Chapter 30

A small opportunity presented itself in 1908. Black Coyote came to visit one spring day as Reuben was framing the new barn. It had been two years since Broken Lance's death. Black Coyote's shorn hair had grown long again, and it was time for a wacipi to honor his father, he said. He asked Reuben's permission for a gathering of Arapaho people beside his creek. Reuben remembered that on the day they'd met over the deer Black Coyote had shot, Black Coyote had told him his people had gathered by the spring for many years.

By now Reuben knew well how the government and some white people continued to take advantage of the natives, and he understood the Indians' resentment. Though settlers had gained a quarter section each of Indian land virtually free, some, including him, had wanted more. What they could not own, others hoped to use. From the beginning white ranchers tried to lease what remained of the Indians' land. Some cattlemen and farmers pastured or planted Indian land and then refused to pay. Capt. A.E. Woodsen, the acting Indian Agent in 1893, tried at first to look out for Indian interests, but found his efforts could not be enforced.

Woodson apparently thought that requiring Indians to stay on their allotments instead of roaming or living more communally would turn them into farmers, so he banned traditional celebrations and forbade more than four families to gather in one place. In 1896 he even banned the traditional Sundance, though thousands of Cheyennes and Arapahos defied the order and gathered at Cantonment in 1901. Reuben had little understanding of traditional Indian ways, and he too wished they would settle down and farm like he and his white neighbors were trying to do.

But neither had Reuben been able to ignore the abuse and the poverty of his Arapaho neighbors, and he knew it was probably unrealistic to expect them to apply themselves to farming as he did. After all, he'd learned to farm from his father, and had grown up assuming that that would be his life. His native neighbors lacked both that experience and the assumptions that drove his determination to succeed on the land.

Reuben considered for a moment. He did have concerns. How many people might show up, and how long would they stay? Where would they camp? Would there be any damage to his pasture or crops? Watongah informed him that in such a traditional gathering, all the clan is invited. Given traveling distances and the poverty in which most of the Arapaho lived, he didn't expect hundreds to come, but who knew? Perhaps many families at least. They would bring what food they had, drink from the spring and not disturb the land. They would gather at summer solstice, so they would not bring tipis. They would sleep under the stars—if they slept at all. They would feast and dance and sing for two days, and then they would go home. He assured Reuben there would be no trouble. Reuben saw no way to say no, so he said yes. He even found himself offering to butcher a yearling steer from his small but growing herd to feed the wacipi crowd.

Yet as summer solstice approached, Reuben's apprehension grew. He knew and trusted Black Coyote, and he could not escape the awareness that he was now prospering on Indian land, including land that had fallen into his hands through what the Arapaho called the "dead Indian act." Yet he was also aware that many Indians had fallen into the grip of alcohol, and he knew that their resentment and discontent was widespread, especially as non-Indians gained title to more and more of their land. But Black Coyote returned the last day of spring to reassure him that there would be no drinking, and that no harm would come to him or his neighbors or to his crops and land. Together they butchered the beef as they had butchered the deer in the winter of Ruth and Reuben's greatest need, cut up the meat and hung it in a tree near the creek to cure.

That afternoon Arapahos began to arrive, some in overloaded rickety wagons, a few on paint ponies, others on foot. Some had brought meat—venison, wild turkey, rabbits, whatever they could find in the dwindling populations of wildlife. Others brought coffee, native turnips and herbs, dough to fry bread. A few brought produce from gardens they had planted with native corn as well as seeds white settlers had brought. Reuben welcomed the early arrivers, then went home to roof his barn. Black Coyote invited Reuben to return with his family that evening to share the feast.

The new house and barn were a good quarter mile from the spring, something Reuben and Ruth often regretted, but they had a good well in the bottom, so they were no longer dependent on spring water. They had also moved the garden to a plot near the new house and had planted a second orchard nearby, though by now the original trees were fifteen years old, and the Westerfields had enjoyed and sold their fruits for years.

Reuben's hammer rang all afternoon. John was now twelve years old, and he worked with his father like a man. Reuben tried to protect him from the most dangerous jobs, such as working on the roof, but John could pick up a whole sheet of tin by himself and boost it up. He kept Reuben supplied with drinking water, nails and any tool he might need, thus keeping the operation running efficiently.

The sun was still high in the western sky when Reuben drove the last nail. He climbed down and went to the house to wash up. He had not mentioned the invitation to Ruth or John, but had been contemplating it all afternoon. He found Ruth busy making bread. "Would you like to join the visitors for supper at the spring?" he asked.

"Yes!" John said immediately. "Let's go!"

Ruth wasn't so sure, partly because her dinner was already planned. Reuben pointed out that she could take freshly baked bread as their contribution to the meal. "It would probably be the best bread they've ever tasted," he said. So when the bread came out of the oven, Ruth wrapped it in a towel and they set out walking up the hill.

When they topped the rise they found scores of people in a big circle around a fire. Women in long dresses worked around the edges, turning meat on sticks. Men sat in a group near the spring. Occasionally one would rise to stir the embers or to feed the fire with another armload of the wood they'd brought. Children chased each other in a game that looked like tag. Smoke drifted their way, and with it the aroma of roasting beef and game.

Black Coyote stood and came to meet the Westerfields. He escorted them to where the men now all stood, and every man extended his hand to each family member. Then Black Coyote introduced the Westerfields to the women, and the ritual was repeated. Meanwhile the kids had ceased their play to watch. Then a boy pealed away from the group and took John by the arm and led him away. He slapped John on the back and ran. The game was on again and John was it.

When the meat was done, everybody gathered around the fire. Black Coyote talked sadly in his language about the father he had lost, then four men circled around a drum to sing an honor song. When the song was done, the women served, and the men and children began to eat.

The sun sank in a crimson western sky. The drummers resumed their positions and the singing and dancing began, the women and a few of the children and men forming a ring around the fire. Reuben and Ruth stood to excuse themselves, Reuben saying it had been a long day of work and they should be heading home. Black Coyote would not hear of it. He insisted they stay. So the Westerfields retreated to the edge of the circle of light to watch. But that was not to be. Soon one of the women came to Ruth, took her by the arm and led her into the circle that danced around the fire.

Then one of the drummers announced a new song. The Westerfields did not understand his words, of course, but the announcement was followed by laughter. Women and girls began searching the dark fringes for a favorite man or boy. That was when John realized that a girl about his age was headed straight for him. "My name is Prairie Star," she said in English. "What is your name?"

"I'm John," the boy mumbled, embarrassed by the attention. Then she had him by the arm and was guiding him into the circle of dancers. Ruth and Reuben watched in amusement. John had shown no interest in girls, and he was acquainted with only the handful of girls who attended the Prairie Valley School. He was clearly uncomfortable with this unexpected encounter. Prairie Star had to almost drag his reluctant feet toward the fire. But by the second time around the fire he looked more relaxed, and by the third round he seemed to be enjoying himself.

That song ended and others followed, and then Reuben became aware that John and Prairie Star were nowhere to be seen. It was only the stars that saw them walk hand in hand into the shadows and to the spring, watched them dip their hands into the water and drink, saw Prairie Star circle her arms around John's waist, draw him close and kiss his lips.

For John it was as if the world had been recreated. Prairie Star was without doubt the loveliest creature he had seen. She was warm and lively, dark eyes sparkling in the glow of the distant fire. He had been completely unprepared when she had left the circle of fire to choose him, but what was happening to him now was a dream he had yet to dream. But what he did know was that the new fire he felt was good, that after this moment he would never be the same. His arms now returned Prairie Star's embrace and they kissed again.

Footsteps were approaching the spring. The pair darted into the shadows on the far side of the creek, then slowed to a walk, hand in hand swishing through lush prairie grasses until they were far from the crowd. But suddenly Prairie Star stopped. "I have to get back to my people," she said. "My mother will be worried, and she might be mad."

John's parents had never been far from his mind either, but whatever trepidation he felt about what they might be thinking he eagerly suppressed. That was the kind of thing one could worry about later. But now later had come. "Yes, we'd better get back," he said. "But how can I see you again?"

"I live an hour's walk west," she said. My mother is Dawn and my father is Arden Breedlove. He doesn't know my mother and I are here. If he was home he probably would not have allowed us to come. But he's off somewhere on what he calls business, whatever that is. So maybe when he's away we can meet again?"

"Yes," John said, startled by the news that the girl he had kissed was the daughter of the man he'd heard stories about. He had no idea how or where they would meet, but he knew they must. From what he had heard about Arden Breedlove, he knew there might be trouble if either of their fathers knew. "We'll have to figure out a way," he said. He drew her close and kissed her again, and then they ran hand in hand through the darkness toward the encampment.

They separated on the far side of the creek and each chose a different route back to the crowd, John circling in the darkness and rejoining his parents from the east. "And where have you been?" his father demanded in a tone that John knew could mean trouble.

"Just talking by the creek," he said, thankful for the darkness that obscured his face, a face he knew would have betrayed his lie.

"Just talking?" his mother asked. "You were with that Indian girl who took you to dance, weren't you?"

"Yes," John said. "Her name is Prairie Star."

"Well, whatever you were doing, it's past time you were in bed," she added sternly. "I'm not going to have you spending the night out here with a bunch of wild Indians. Let's go home." Down the hill they trudged, their footsteps guided by the stars, nobody speaking a word.

When they reached the house, John went straight to his room, eager to avoid further interrogation. But he found that sleep would not come. In spite of a long day in the sun, a long day of man's work, it was the awakening of the man in the boy that kept him from sleep, that and the regular beat of the drums that resonated through his open window. He imagined Prairie Star's slender body inching along to the beat, her dark eyes reflecting the fire he'd felt on her lips. It seemed he could still feel her lithe body in his arms, her lips burning into his. Before tonight he had given not a single second thought to any girl he knew. But tonight everything had changed.

Across the Cimarron

CHAPTER 31

Even though they were separated by only four miles, there was no easy way for John and Prairie Star to see each other. Both were aware that their fathers were not on friendly terms, so it was not likely the families would meet. Once in August John sneaked away after bedtime on a moonlit night and ran across the prairies and fields to Prairie Star's house. When he came within sight he slackened his pace and moved stealthily amongst the shadows until he reached the house. He had never been inside the house, but his father had described the structure he'd built, so John knew it consisted of three rooms, a kitchen, a sitting room and a bedroom, with a small loft room in the attic. That would likely be where Prairie Star slept, so on the way he'd thought of ways to get her attention if she had gone to bed. He'd stopped at the spring for a pocketful of pebbles he figured he could chunk at the window if all else failed.

He peeked in the window. Prairie Star and her mother sat by the lamp, darning socks. Her father was nowhere to be seen. Now John had only to be noticed by Prairie Star, but not by her mother. Peering through the edge of the window he scratched at the glass. No response. He scratched harder, then gently pecked at the glass with his knuckle. Both mother and daughter glanced up, but went on with their work. He tapped a bit harder and the two glanced directly at the window with puzzled looks on their faces. The mother spoke and lay her work aside. She got up from her rocking chair and moved toward the door.

She opened the door and stepped out into the moonlight. Now John rapped more loudly and made himself completely visible in the window. Prairie Star looked up and her mouth fell open. She looked toward the open door, then waved. The mother came back in, said something else, then resumed her work.

John waited in the shadows, wondering if Prairie Star would come. At last she spoke to her mother, got up and headed for the door. As soon as the door was closed she streaked around the house to where John waited. She threw her arms around him and they kissed. "I wanted to see you," he said. "I think about you all the time."

"And I think of you," she replied. "I told my mother I was going to the outhouse, so I only have a minute. How will we meet again?"

"I could come again on the next full moon," John said. "But I can't come until Mom and Dad are in bed."

"I'll watch for you," she said, "but be careful. My father may be home." She kissed him long, embracing him in her strong slender arms. "Now you'd better go. Until next full moon!"

John turned and ran again down the moonlit trail, across scraps of still unbroken prairie and plowed wheat fields, not slowing until the cottonwood grove came into view. He slowed to a trot, then to a walk so that when he opened the door his panting had ceased. Very slowly he crept across the floor, avoiding the boards that squeaked, stripped off his clothes and fell into bed. The night was still hot, especially in the house, but his body burned with other heat.

Before the next full moon, school began. On the second day the teacher announced that in October the Prairie Valley students would visit Mulberry Grove for a spelling bee, so they must begin to prepare. Only later did John remember that the purpose of the proposed visit was a spelling contest; what he had heard was the name Mulberry Grove—Prairie Star's school.

And so it went. Only rarely did they see each other, and then usually briefly or in non-intimate circumstances, until the Saturday night the following summer when John and his folks stepped out of the general store in Okeene, arms full of provisions they had traded eggs and cream to buy, and who should be coming in but Prairie Star and her parents. It was also the first time Reuben and Arden had met for several years, and Ruth and Dawn had never been introduced. Reuben recovered from the unexpected encounter as quickly as he could. "Good evening," he said to Arden, his full arms providing an excuse not to shake hands, then turned to Dawn. "I don't believe you've met my wife, Ruth," he said. "And this is our son John."

"It's nice to meet you," Ruth said.

"And I know about John," Dawn said. "Prairie Star told me they were friends."

"Is that right?" Arden boomed. "Since when?"

"We met at the spelling bee," John squeaked, immediately fearing that the half truth would be exposed.

Prairie Star's twinkling eyes met John's. She extended her hand. "It's very nice to see you," she said.

"Well, we'd better get these things to the wagon," Reuben said, stepping off the boardwalk. When they were leaving the lights of town Reuben grilled John about Prairie Star. His answers were vague and brief.

Months passed, and then years. John and Prairie Star both finished eighth grade, and John began the work of a man, all day in the fields, working with the livestock and at his father's side at the forge. By now they had grown their herd to a dozen cows and a bull, a sow and a boar to produce pigs for meat and for sale and four strong mares to pull the plow and other farm implements. They still did not have a stud, so one fine spring day when Molly came into heat and Reuben happened to be helping a neighbor frame a barn, John was dispatched to take the mare to Breedlove to be serviced.

He saddled the mare and rode west. He and Prairie Star had not seen each other since late fall. It had finally become impossible to keep secret that he loved Prairie Star, and little by little he had revealed that information to his parents. Reuben was not pleased, not only because Prairie Star's aging father was a ruffian, a drinker and a gambler, but also her mother was an Indian. Reuben made little of that fact, his main objection being to Arden. But it had long ago become public knowledge that Bertram was his brother, and now to top that off, his son was enchanted by an Indian girl. Bertram and Sally had long since acquired their own farm down the river and were doing as well as most of the neighbors, and clearly Arden too had succeeded in his own way. Reuben knew that it was futile to try to squelch the relationship, and he also knew how few eligible young women there were in the neighborhood. Yet, to John it was clear that his father disapproved.

When he rode into the Breedlove yard all was quiet. He tied Molly to the rail and knocked at the door. Dawn Breedlove answered, her hands covered to the elbows with the bread dough she was kneading. "Is Mr. Breedlove here," he asked. "I've brought a mare."

"I'm afraid he's not here," Mrs. Breedlove replied. "He's off to town. But Prairie Star is in the garden. She can give you a hand if you need it, and you can settle up with Arden later." John thanked her and headed toward the garden, the familiar flame rising in his body.

Prairie Star saw him coming and tossed aside her hoe. She ran and jumped into his arms. "It's been so long since you've come, I thought you'd forgotten about me," she said. "I've missed you so." For answer he drew her tight and they kissed again and again.

Finally he remembered why he'd come. "I brought a mare to see old Boomer," he said sheepishly.

"And what do you think they might do?" she asked with a sly grin.

"I guess we'll find out," he said. He broke free and went to lead Molly to the stallion's pen. Boomer had long since become aware of her presence, of course. He was pacing the rail fence, his big head bobbing, whinnying with desire. John pulled off Molly's saddle and led her to the gate. Prairie Star swung the gate open and she galloped in. And they were off, charging the length of the corral, spinning in a cloud of dust and back. John and Prairie Star went into the barn to watch. For several minutes the horses raced and rampaged until finally Molly bolted to a stop and immediately Boomer mounted her, biting her neck as he delivered what Molly had come for.

John turned to Prairie Star and looked long into her yearning eyes. Then suddenly they were in hot embrace and then they were in the hay, rolling and kissing. Her dress came up above her waist and the desire that had grown in both young bodies for half a dozen years could no longer be repressed. They loved as if their lives depended upon it, for they did, and finally when it was over they rolled onto their backs but still in each others' arms, hearts pounding, breath blowing, sweat rolling down faces and necks into the hay, the dust they'd stirred filtering down through the shaft of sunlight that illuminated the pile of hay where their longing had finally been without reservation expressed.

"I love you Prairie Star," John murmured. "I will love you forever. I want you to marry me. I want your love every day for the rest of my life."

"Oh John," Prairie Star whispered. "Of course I'll marry you. But," she added, "of course my father will say no."

"I don't care what he says, my love," John replied. "If we have to go away to be together we will go away. Being with you is the only thing that matters." And so they lay long in that sweet embrace, until Boomer's frantic whinnying told them that he was about to add insurance that another foal would be on its way. When they looked up, Arden Breedlove was framed in the doorway.

"What is this!" he yelled. Get your pants on and get your damned horse and get off my place," he said to John. He grabbed him by the arm and jerked him up. "And you," he said to Prairie Star, "get yourself to the house. I'll deal with you later."

"You can't stop us from loving each other," John blurted. "We are going to be married, no matter what anybody says." Prairie Star was on her feet, her expression confused and hurt and afraid. "And don't you lay a hand on Prairie Star," John said to Breedlove. "If you do, you will answer to me."

Breedlove laughed. "Don't scare me, pipsqueak," he said. "Now get your horse and get off the place. By the way, tell your old man that this service is free, but it will be his last." He turned and followed Prairie Star toward the house.

Across the Cimarron

CHAPTER 32

Looking back, Reuben regretted having made it so difficult for John to be with Prairie Star. After all, they were eighteen, fully grown and ready for a life together. But even if he and Ruth had not stood in the way, Arden Breedlove certainly did, even threatening John when he found them together again in the woods that fall. John had told Reuben and Ruth that he intended to marry Prairie Star, and even though they knew there was nothing they could do to prevent the union, Reuben persuaded John to wait. After all, they were still young and John had no way to support a wife. There was no more free Indian land to be had, so getting a foothold would require some help. Reuben promised that if they waited until they were twenty-one, he would help them set up a place of their own, maybe build a house on the original homestead near the spring where the twelve year olds had met, even give them a start with livestock. John could not argue that he was prepared to support a wife and perhaps a family, and though he feared that Prairie Star would endure more years of ill-treatment from her father, he finally agreed to wait.

For Reuben the next three years were a blur of struggle and work, but also a time in which they began new enterprises and continued to till more crops and increase their herd of cows. A week after Breedlove found John and Prairie Star together in the barn, war broke out in Europe. Nobody imagined that it would ever impact this community of settlers on Cheyenne Arapaho land; in fact President Wilson announced that the United States would remain neutral. And on the farm the distant war brought greater prosperity. The price of wheat shot up, for a time reaching the unimaginable price of three dollars a bushel, and crops were good. For the first time in twenty-one years on the Cimarron, the

Westerfields didn't worry about making ends meet. Reuben wasn't ready to do something as foolish as a couple of neighbors—rush out and buy an internal combustion powered tractor or car, but the wolf was from the door and they had money in the bank.

For John, the years dragged by, Reuben knew, like a lifetime in purgatory, except for more frequent opportunities to see Prairie Star. Increasingly Arden Breedlove was away, at one point even catching a train to Mexico with a group of land speculators. Arden had never taken to farming, though he'd finally paid a neighbor to fence his land so he could run a small herd of cows along with his breeding stock. When Breedlove was away, Prairie Star invariably also slipped away and came to meet John. By now they both had horses of their own, so they sometimes met at the spring and rode together along the river. Eventually they began to join Reuben and Ruth around the kitchen table for meals.

After a time all of Reuben's misgivings slipped away. He saw that Prairie Star was as intelligent, hardworking and pleasant as she was beautiful. And yet he was glad they would not marry soon, giving John time to earn his independence before he yielded that to another. So Reuben and John worked side by side, planting alfalfa, mowing and hauling in hay, setting up bee hives so they could add honey to the fruit and eggs they sold in town, planting a field of cane and joining with neighbors each fall to make sorghum for winter and for sale.

Bertram and Sally's son Tom also had his own horse, and on Sunday afternoons he often rode over for a lesson on the violin. He readily took to the instrument, and before long was playing it in church as well as at dances in the Negro community. Not to be outdone, John at last took up the guitar. Reuben had encouraged him to learn one or the other of his instruments when John was a small child, but perhaps he pushed too hard, and John had shied away. Now John decided to make the guitar his own—partly because Prairie Star so enjoyed hearing him sing and play. And now the two cousins were playing together, which drew them closer than they had ever been.

The future looked bright. Prairie Star and John set their wedding date for June. And then the United States entered the Great War. In January 1917, Germany began sinking merchant ships with its submarines. In February the president broke off relations with Germany, but he seemed still determined to keep the U.S. out of the war. But when the seventh American ship was sunk, the die was cast. On the sixth of April Congress declared war on Germany. Few American men volunteered to fight this distant and unpopular war, so on May 18 Congress passed the Selective Service Act, which would apply to all men aged twenty-one to thirty-one. John had just celebrated his twenty-first birthday. He was among the first round of nearly three million men drafted to fight the war.

Tom Washington was also twenty-one, but he was not selected in the first round. There was little question that he would be drafted sooner or later, so when John turned himself in for induction, Tom went along as a volunteer. The cousins had grown close, and they assumed that they would now fight the Germans together. Of course that was not to be. They might have learned from their own history, by the fact that state government had torn them apart at the end of first grade because Tom was a Negro. Now they learned that the U.S. Army was also segregated. They rode the train together to Oklahoma City for induction, but they would not see each other again until they came home from war.

By fall John was on a ship headed for France, part of the first wave of what would eventually be ten thousand new soldiers each day, consigned to fight in long-stalemated trench warfare until the final offensive. The winter of 1917 was the worst part for John. Lying in a muddy trench and subsisting on sometimes rancid food, watching countless comrades blown to bits by German shells, he found himself almost envying the dead. What he could not do was allow himself to think about Prairie Star, or to wonder what she was doing, or especially to imagine the alternative life for which he had waited for nearly a decade, to be lying not in a cold muddy trench, but in her warm enveloping arms.

He did sometimes think about Tom. In a rare letter from home he learned that Tom was somewhere in Virginia, loading ships with the tools of war. At least he was safe from German tanks, though he knew Tom would not be happy that he was not deemed worthy to fight because of the color of his skin.

When the Armistice was finally signed on November 11, 1918, John felt like a different man. His body was gaunt, his mind numb. He had grown so accustomed to death that he paid it little heed. His ears rang permanently from the burst of shells. A nasty fungus grew between his toes. At last he boarded a ship once more in January 1919. He had a hot shower and got medicine for his feet. The mess hall served all the hot food he could eat. He took his turn in the barber chair. And once again when he looked in a mirror, he saw somebody he almost recognized. It was an older man, to be sure. Old, though not yet twenty-three.

The journey home seemed interminable, long days and nights at sea, lulled to the best sleep he'd had in two years in a narrow bunk, one of hundreds in a merchant ship that rolled and creaked with the waves until daylight, then a long day of waiting for his turn in the bunk until at last the ship docked in the middle of the night. They were awakened and ordered off and transported to a railroad yard, where he boarded a long troop train, thousands of veterans, some wounded, some on crutches or crazed, most mute, staring out the window as the country unfolded on their way west, across a fertile plain, through town after town, crawling through mountain gaps, finally emerging in the hills of his father's Tennessee. The train stopped in most every town and somebody got off. Sometimes they were met by mothers and fathers or lovers and friends, sometimes they shouldered their duffle bags and trudged into darkness alone.

After many nights and days, and on the last of several trains, John finally stepped out into the February sunshine in Okeene. Prairie Star ran to meet him and leapt into his arms, tears of relief and joy streaming down her cheeks. Waiting behind her for their turn were his mother and father, who it seemed to him had aged at least as much as he while he was gone. He carried his bag to the buggy and they got in and drove toward the Cimarron. He had seen the river when they crossed on the train, but he would not be home until he sat down with Prairie Star on its bank.

Sometimes it seemed to all of them as if they'd just met for the first time. There was awkwardness in conversation; John sometimes had nothing to say. He seemed distant, responding to their love, but almost as a stranger might have done. They did not press him for details of where he had been and what he had seen; they had read enough of that in the newspapers. Neither did John speak freely about his two years away, though he and Tom got together every chance they had. They all realized that there were things that only those who had experienced them could share, but they sensed that sharing them was probably necessary.

Even with Prairie Star he sometimes found himself thinking of other things. She was affectionate as always, and the passion of old was frequently aroused. But two weeks passed, and he had said nothing about marriage. Finally, sitting on a bale of hay in the barn, she brought it up. "Do you still want to marry me John?" she asked.

"Yes, of course," he replied. "When, do you think?"

"Today," she said with a relieved laugh, "or tomorrow at the latest."

Now it was his turn to laugh. "OK," he said, "I agree. Let's get married this afternoon." They shared a long sweet kiss, then just held each other in embrace.

"But probably our families will want a real wedding," she said, breaking the spell. "After all, we're the only chance they will have."

So they began to speak in practical terms about the life they would begin together, about setting a date and what sort of wedding they would have, about building a house, and finally about the father from whom she was largely estranged. "We need to have him there," John said firmly. "I will invite him myself, and if necessary I'll drag him there." They decided to marry on the hill by the spring, in the shade of the cottonwoods where they had shared the first kiss. They decided on April. They didn't want to wait any longer, but that would give them a few weeks to prepare. "What day in April?" John asked. And then he answered his own question. "The nineteenth, of course," he said, "the day our fathers claimed this land."

And so on April 19, neighbors gathered on the hill between the blossoming fruit trees and the spring. A fattened pig was roasting over coals and there was a jug of Reuben's homemade wine. The Washingtons and a few other neighbors from downriver were there, and of course Tom brought not only his fiddle, but his new fiancée, Betsy, the youngest daughter of the couple who had camped behind Reuben the night before the run. The Westerfields' first neighbors, the Webers, came early to help with preparations, and one by one most of the families who had settled along the river arrived. Prairie Star's aging grandfather, Black Coyote, was there, and so was her mother, Dawn. It was nearly time for the ceremony to begin, and so far Arden Breedlove had not appeared. But then those waiting saw a small cloud of dust appear on the western horizon, which materialized into a galloping horse. Two minutes more and he was there, reining the horse hard as always, and sliding down. Breedlove strode straight toward the young couple, though rather stiffly at age seventy-one, limping more noticeably than in earlier days.

Nobody knew what might happen next. But when he reached his daughter and her groom he paused, gazed a moment into John's unflinching eyes and extended his hand. "Take good care of my daughter," he said. He embraced Prairie Star. The whole assembly broke into clapping and cheers. As the wave of relief faded away, Tom picked up his fiddle and began to play.

CHAPTER 33

That was all so long ago, and sometimes when Reuben thought back over those earlier years he realized that he had begun to question his memory. Had things really happened as he remembered them, or had they perhaps morphed in his mind into narratives that likely had grown beyond reality but whose details and images had grown hazy and dim. Hazy and dim like this day. There had been no sign of sun for three days now, but this darkest of days was growing darker. If he remembered right, Highway 81 was three miles down river from the county bridge; he only hoped they would reach it before dark. If there was any bridge that had survived the flood and remained open, surely that would be it.

Ruth had relapsed into the stupor that might have been sleep, and Reuben now fought to keep his eyes open, to maintain the vigilance he knew would be required if they were to save themselves. Several times he found himself nodding off; he was shocked to catch himself wondering whether that might be all right, maybe the best thing to do. But he could not. For eighty-nine years he had never yielded to weakness, never in all the times that he was tempted to surrender as the easy way out. He had always known without thinking about it that to waver was to fail.

But he did nod off. Suddenly his eyes jerked open and reality came rushing back. It was nearly dark, but less than a quarter mile ahead, the long, low Highway 81 bridge stretched across the horizon. He grabbed Ruth's arm and shook it hard. "Wake up!" he shouted. "Here comes the bridge. We have to make a plan to get out." Ruth's eyes opened, but she did not move. He shook her again, then grasped below her shoulders and tugged to raise her up.

When she was seated he began frantically scanning what lay ahead. It appeared that water was no more than a couple of feet below the deck. The new bridge had concrete posts and rails, so getting out looked easy compared to the county bridge where they had failed. They would simply float slowly to the bridge, stand up and be borne directly against the rail. He would lift Ruth over, then climb over himself, and they would be saved. "This is it," he said to Ruth. "We're going to get out here!" He described to her the process he saw in his mind. She did not reply, but neither did she proclaim likely failure in advance as she had done before. He hoped that meant she shared his confidence that this time they would succeed.

The bridge loomed closer, perhaps an eighth of a mile. But now he saw what he had not seen before. They were moving across the river at least as fast as they were floating down. When he had first spotted the bridge they were headed for its center. Now they were being swept toward the south end. And then he saw why. The road leading to the bridge from the south had been washed away. The river filled the valley to the south as far as the fading light would permit him to see.

If only he had an oar, or a pole of some kind, anything to nudge the floating chicken house back toward the center. There was nothing. Strange that in a long day on the swollen river not a single tool he might use had come within reach. So there was nothing he could do, nothing but wait. Would they hit the bridge, or would the current sweep them past the abutment, across the washed out roadbed and on down the river? If they missed this opportunity, the next bridge must be at least twenty miles away.

Now it was becoming apparent; there was no way they would hit the bridge. The bridge was actually diverting the water. The mile-wide river was funneling through the gap at its end! Reuben's heart sank, but he did not tell Ruth what he had concluded. She would see it soon enough. Anyway, there was nothing to say but that the latest hope was likely dashed.

Now the river raged as the great flood waters sucked into the funnel, but over the roar Reuben heard a voice. Yes, two figures stood where the road disappeared in roiling flood. The hen house rocked and dipped as it rushed toward the funnel's mouth, and he dared not stand on the slippery roof. He raised to his knees, waving his arms. "Hello!" he shouted as loud as his dry, hoarse throat would permit. "We need help! Hello! Do you see us out here?" The muffled voices continued their conversation. The speakers did not glance toward the scrap of debris sweeping into the vortex in gathering darkness.

The last post of the bridge abutment was so close! If only he had a rope. It was less than twenty feet away, but it may as well have been a mile. Now they were in the raging current sweeping past the bridge, the chicken house churning and tilting as if after a long day of upright sailing it would finally capsize. Reuben gripped the roof edge with one hand and Ruth with the other as the bridge rushed by.

Past the constriction the foamy waters calmed, and the rocking subsided. Reuben glanced back at the silhouette blackened against the western sky. With light fading, he could no longer hide from himself that Ruth might have been right. They weren't likely to get out alive. Without a word she slumped back to the roof and closed her eyes, leaving Reuben alone to face the falling darkness. His stomach was collapsing with hunger. His muscles ached with stiffness and fatigue. But most of all his mouth and throat were so dry that, especially after the exertion of his feeble shouts, even breathing had become difficult. He eyed the roiling water, no longer brown but black, the water that had become the only reality of life. He dipped his hand into the river and drank.

Across the Cimarron

CHAPTER 34

Reuben awoke with a start. His stomach was heaving. He dragged himself to the edge and retched. The sky was black, not a single star. The only relief from blackness was the white collar of Ruth's dress beneath her rain coat. Her body had slipped a ways down the roof. He edged back toward her and took her hand. It was cold. He felt her wrist. The pulse was there, but weak. He grasped below her shoulders and dragged her back to the peak. She did not awake.

Reuben tried to focus on their dilemma, turning over possibilities for rescue that now seemed unlikely at best, but he found he couldn't concentrate. Even under good circumstances these days he'd found himself dwelling in the past, his aging mind replaying certain stories irrepressibly. And present circumstances were nothing if not bleak.

The specter of the lost first son invariably rose to consciousness, but now it came to him that if Jacob had lived he would be not the frail baby of memory, but an aging man. How old would he be? Sixty-four if he had lived. Who knew how that life might have played out, how many grandchildren he and Ruth might have, if only they'd had a milk cow. There was no way to know if that would have saved Jacob, but Reuben had never for a moment convinced himself otherwise. He'd bought a gun with money that could have bought a cow. The self indictment was not entirely rational, he knew. He could also have bought the Dugans' cow if he hadn't been struck by the rattlesnake that took the money from chopping firewood. As always memory tortured his mind, but he was powerless to close the book.

In some ways the first great tragedy was overwhelmed by the second, by the day Joseph was thrown from the horse. Jacob had lived little more than a month, and that without strength or health. He'd really never had a chance. Joseph, on the other hand, was the picture of health—tall, strong, good looking, smart—everything one might hope for in a son or grandson. To lose him to a worthless horse was a tragedy that could have been avoided, if not for the one flaw in Joseph's character, the stubborn streak that made him think he could do anything he chose to do, even where others had failed. But where did he get this mindset, Reuben always had to remind himself. One reason he'd loved Joe so much was that the boy reminded him of himself.

If life had taught him anything, Reuben had learned how callously it displays the ironies it doles out. A more primitive mind might have been forgiven the conclusion that some angry or vengeful god pulled certain strings to punish men for their mistakes, or perhaps just to taunt them with cruel displays of power. Why was it that in this land of promise, he and Ruth, Bertram and Sally, even Arden and Dawn Breedlove, should be limited to one child each? And to top it off, the wild horse Joseph insisted on riding was the grandson of Boomer, the offspring of the mare he had sent John to be serviced by Breedlove's stud.

Unable to redirect his mind to plans for salvation, Reuben tried to focus on better memories, on the fact that life had dealt him many lucky cards along with the bad. In many ways, his life had been charmed. Finding Ruth was the best thing that had happened to him. Even though her own sorrows and disappointments had taken a deep toll on her mind, she had been a good companion and partner. When she was haunted by blue devils, or when she sensed that Reuben was feeling low, she sometimes begged him to bring out an instrument and play. That never failed to raise their spirits, at least for a time. No, he couldn't have asked for a better wife.

But recognition of his good fortune, surviving and thriving on free land, could not drive out the thing that haunted his brain as much as the death of sons—the loss of the down-river claim. Especially after he and Ruth visited the place during the great drought and found it thriving, he couldn't shake either the resentment he felt over this injustice, or the wistful thoughts of what might have been. All the subsequent chapters of his life would have taken different turns he knew, if he could have held that claim. He fought off the feelings by reminding himself that not many penniless men in history had been handed a farm, even a marginal farm, just for the taking, even if that taking—and holding—had required more guts and hard work than most men could have mustered. Hard red land, yes, but eventually they had prospered there. They had mostly lived well. After the first years they'd had more than enough good food. They'd been blessed with long lives, if that was a blessing. And in later years they'd enjoyed the company and support of John and Prairie Star, even as they shared their grief.

And there was so much more. A lot of living can be crammed into eighty-nine years, so much tragedy and struggle, but bookcased with pleasure and joy. Now floating along on a black river under a dark sky, Reuben struggled to keep his mind awake with memories, even uninvited memories he ordinarily sought to suppress. He must remain awake just in case some unforeseen opportunity presented itself through which they might be saved.

Reuben tried to picture their first dwellings, the dugout that long ago had collapsed, leaving only a grassy depression in the edge of the bluff he had climbed, the sod house that also had slowly sunk back into the earth from which it came, now merely a mound that resembled a giant's grave. Parts of the log house still stood, though it had not been used for decades. The fine framed house was now gone too, but that image was still too fresh to exactly be called a memory. It had happened only this morning, he realized with shock, if in fact the lightning strike and the fire had actually occurred, and if it had occurred in this present life. But here they were, floating down the Cimarron on the chicken house roof, so everything he recalled from this longest day must actually have transpired. This day too had formed a chapter in memory.

He kept himself awake by picturing all the houses he'd built for other people, most of wood, a couple with concrete blocks and stone. How many? Beginning in Wichita, then helping Peter Weber, then the house for Arden Breedlove, and including helping John and Prairie Star, there must have been a dozen or more. And all without major incident except for the day he fell off the roof of a house he was building for the Renshaws and broke his collar bone. He paid a quack doctor to set it, but a day later the pain was so great he could tell by feel that it wasn't right. With Bertram's help he had reset it himself, and finally it had healed.

There was the mad dog that came side-winding down Bertram and Sally's driveway one July day when he was helping Bertram build his barn. If only he'd had the gun he could have shot the thing before it bit Tom. The only way anybody had to treat rabies in those days was with a mad stone. He'd gone all the way to Okeene to borrow it from somebody a neighbor had heard about. When he got back Tom seemed at the door of death. They strapped the boy to the bed and bound the stone to his temple, where it remained for three days. When Tom awoke Reuben was there, playing the fiddle. Tom's first request, even before he asked for a glass of water, was that Reuben teach him to play. They knew then that Tom would live.

But living had never been easy. Just when they felt they were finally secure after forty years of hard work, along came the Great Depression, accompanied by drought and dust. Wheat sold for as little as twenty-five cents a bushel in those years, less than it cost to grow it and ship it to market. So many neighbors lost out in the thirties, so much struggle and pain.

Reuben's mind galloped aimlessly across nearly nine decades of life, but he was aware that in important ways the fulcrum that divided future orientation from past came in 1938, when Joseph died. With his only grandchild gone, it was the end of his line. All that he and Ruth and John and Prairie Star had worked so hard for would die with them. So in a way he too had died that lovely day nineteen years ago. He had continued to go through all the necessary motions, had continued to work and even to make music when asked and to enjoy life's little pleasures as they came, but nothing was ever quite the same.

He had been to many funerals since then, Bertram and Sally, both of the Webers, Black Coyote, even Arden Breedlove, who had lived a life as long as Reuben's but had now been dead for maybe twenty years. Perhaps it was not just the death of Joseph, but the death of most everybody with whom he'd shared the most active years of his life that crowded the later decades from the reels that played and replayed in his mind.

And now, death seemed not so bad. In any case it was unavoidable, and perhaps their time had come. If so, then so be it. Why continue what seemed a losing battle? Reuben closed his eyes.

Across the Cimarron

CHAPTER 35

The jolt nearly knocked Reuben from his perch. Apparently the ark had hit something that brought it to an abrupt halt. Dozing, he had slipped precariously close to the roof's lower edge. Water was lapping at the edge, which at the moment was downriver and listing at a sharper angle than before.

He felt sick again, whether from the water he'd drunk or from hunger and fatigue, or from a combination of factors, he could not tell. He felt rumbling in his guts, and now he could hear it too.

How much time had passed, Reuben had no idea. In the absence of stars and moon the night was black as tar. He could barely make out the ribbon of white below Ruth's chin. He grabbed her wrist and felt again for pulse. It was still there, a low ebb.

So what to do now? Clearly their progress down the river had stopped, but he didn't know why. Then he remembered the matches. He felt under his slicker in his overalls pocket. They felt dry. He brought one out and struck it on a button of his fly. He cupped the flame in his other hand and held the light near Ruth's face. It seemed relaxed, void of tension, but perhaps nearly void of life. He moved the match to the edge of the roof. There was nothing to see but foamy brown, licking gently at the shingles. Judging by the tilt of the roof he decided that whatever they had hit was likely far below water. The building bobbed and ebbed against the obstacle, tilting and leveling, tilting and leveling again.

Might the chicken house go over on its side and dump them in? He moved back toward the peak to balance the structure on the upriver side. He tried hard to think, to marshal weak

resources to address the new problem at hand. He tried to picture
what might lay at the base of their craft. He finally concluded
that, as was often the case, his options were narrowed to two. He
could do nothing and wait for morning—or death—to come, or
he could venture into the river and see whether the object that
had arrested their progress might be used to advantage.

If he slipped into the water, there was a chance he would be
carried away, leaving Ruth marooned alone. She lay near the top
of the incline, so he was fairly sure the structure would not topple
if he got off. He put his hand into the water. It was cold. After all,
it had fallen over the past two days as a cold rain, and there had
been no sun to warm it. He shuddered at the very thought of
venturing in. If only he had something with which to probe.

Without reaching a firm conclusion or forming an action
plan, Reuben slipped off his raincoat and spread it over Ruth. If
he didn't come back, at least she'd be warm if somebody found
her when the sun came up. He unbuckled his overshoes and took
them off, then did the same with brogans and overalls. He looped
a suspender through the shoe laces and overshoe buckles to bind
everything together, then hooked the suspender over Ruth's arm.
Now he was in his underwear, a square of light in the darkness.
He scooted again toward the edge and lowered himself into the
icy water.

His foot encountered resistance. He tapped the thing and felt
pain. He probed more gently. It was a barbed wire fence! Instantly
the image of Palmer returned to his mind. The railroad man had
saved himself on Reuben's fence; perhaps this was the rescue
Reuben had been hoping for. He dipped lower into the water.
Another wire. He had to be within a foot or two of earth. He
slipped deeper, now gripping the edge of the roof in his shaking
hands. His feet hit muddy earth.

If only there was light. Even the feeblest light of stars might
tell him whether the fence led one way or the other to higher
ground. The rain had been stopped for hours, and he guessed the
river level had peaked and would eventually be going down. If
only he could follow the fence to a protruding island—or better
yet, to a bank. There was no way to know which bank they might
be closer to, but it didn't really matter. All that mattered was

gaining land, and then finding water to drink and help to survive. Now that his bare feet were on earth, he began to inch along the fence. The chicken house might have been the largest object the fence had collected, but it was by no means the only thing. Every manner of debris was trapped by the wires. He stumbled and caught himself, the barbs tearing his hand. He was up to his chest, then up to his neck, and then he could go no farther. He turned around and worked his way slowly back toward Ruth, trying to remember the rubble that lay in his path, moving slowly to avoid tripping again or tearing his feet and legs.

At last he reached the building. He felt for its bottom boards and found that only the top wire held it fast, and that hold was tenuous. He proceeded down the fence the other way. Soon he was in water only to his belly, then only to his hips. Elated, he moved on, edging ever farther from the bobbing lifeboat. But then he was back to his belly again, then to his chest, and then to his chin. Again, he could go no farther. He had apparently passed the high point and would not find land. Deflated, he worked his way back. He found a place where the wire was loose, broken perhaps by some other floating junk. He pulled until he found an end, then worked his way up the wire some twenty feet. Grasping it in both hands he began to bend, one way, then the other. He had broken wire this way many times when he had found himself without pliers and with wire that needed to be cut. But that was on dry land. Wire eventually broke because of friction and heat fatigue. Under water the process could take much longer. He raised the ends out of the water and continued to bend. Finally one strand snapped, and soon the other. Now at last he had a tool, but what good it might do he did not know. If they passed a tree or some other stationary object, perhaps they could moor their craft.

Before ascending the roof he wrapped an end of the wire around a protruding nail head at the peak of the roof. Then he felt his way back to the lower side to pull himself up. He found he lacked the strength. He tried again and again, stopped to rest and tried again. His arms were too fatigued for the job, his whole body shaking now with cold. The only thing left was to climb the fence. He found the post, put his foot on the top wire and pulled at the roof again. Just as he heaved himself over the staple gave way, the wire slipped and the chicken house was freed of its anchor and resumed its slow downriver bob. Gripping the mossy shingles he dragged himself to the peak and collapsed in utter exhaustion. His heart pounded and his head was on fire.

When his breathing had slowed Reuben found his clothing and pulled it back on with trembling hands. Only then did he realize how chilled he had become. Exertion had kept his body temperature steady, but in relaxation his limbs shook almost beyond control and he could not stop the chattering of his teeth. His raincoat firmly cinched at his chin, he stretched out beside Ruth and encircled her in his arms.

When the shivering subsided at last, Reuben once again began to address their plight. If they survived the night, it would not be without sleep. What if they hit something else and the chicken house tipped and dumped them into the muddy water? He raised himself weakly and found the loose end of the barbed wire. Carefully he wrapped it around Ruth, then around himself, then found another nail head on the opposite edge of the roof and twisted it tight. He wrapped his arms around Ruth and drew her close. So long as the roof remained upright they would stay above water. Tomorrow somebody would find them, dead or alive. Reuben again closed his eyes.

CHAPTER 36

Now that he had determined to sleep, sleep would not come. It seemed that behind his closed lids, his eyes flashed with prisms of colored light. He tried to think, to calm his agitated mind. He felt his forehead and found it hot with perspiration. For hours he had kept his mind occupied with memories of the past and strategies to confront the present. But the past was exhausted, and the present offered little hope—certainly no viable plan. Looking toward the future, what remained of this night and what tomorrow might bring, seemed a futile exercise, even had he been able to focus. He tried to dwell on things that had sometimes brought him comfort, tried to avoid more pain.

The river was bearing them on, ever nearer his long lost claim, and even though those memories always brought mostly pain, his mind refused to relinquish the images of what might have been. He had seen the place just twice, and then briefly, most recently twenty years ago. And yet it seemed as real as the land where he and Ruth had invested sixty-five years, perhaps because he had so often imagined how life might have been different there. It was impossible to know what sorrow or tragedy that other life might have brought, sorrows he had avoided on the road he had taken. Such things were beyond imagination. What he did see in the path from which he had been diverted was greater success, an easier life, and most of all, the possibility that he and Ruth might have dodged the worst of what fate had dealt.

But no use dwelling on any of that. They had left the living of that life behind now, and he found comfort in dreams of the other life in the promised land they had lost. The images were in vivid color, the greens of pastures and trees, the prairie flowers that were in full bloom that April day so long ago and no doubt were again this night, the dark richness of the soil. Funny how even the house he and Ruth had found when they visited that Saturday afternoon in the middle of the great drought was as he imagined it should be, almost the house that he had foreseen, nestled just right on the slope amongst the cottonwoods and oaks, the long view across fields and orchards and pastures to the Cimarron.

Gradually Reuben's aching muscles yielded their tension. The slow bobbing of the roof and the little lapping sound of gentle waves against the wall, even the subtle churning of the water that surrounded them, all of this was comforting now. The worries about their predicament melted away into a kind of sleep. Somehow everything would turn out all right, as in the end it always had. And so on they floated, through the darkness until the clouds at last began to clear and familiar stars appeared. There was no moon, but the stars were enough. If anybody had been watching, the scene would have been nothing if not peaceful, a loving couple drifting along in a deep embrace, at rest, waiting for the dawn to come.

And then the first ray of light appeared in the east. Only those who were watching closely would have seen it, not yet a hint of rose, but only a sliver on the eastern horizon, just enough light that a keen observer could make out the patterns of hill and tree, and of course water. But then in the blink of an eye almost, the light grew stronger and the morning unfolded, now a tint of pink on the placid foamy flow, but almost immediately an array of brilliant pulsing streaks across the last wisps of cloud.

Where were they now? They had left the place they had known so well far behind, as if in twenty-four hours they had crossed some great ocean, rather than a mere forty or fifty miles of a flooding Cimarron. Reuben squinted into the growing light, which seemed too bright for such an early hour, so bright it nearly blinded his faded eyes. The last of the clouds had sailed away, and the eastern sky was now fiery red. Details of the river banks came into sharp focus, though facing the blinding light, those details were difficult to read. Reuben's exhausted eyes swept slowly along the western bank as far back as he could see, to a point that was only water, but water that itself now reflected the brilliance of the sky, then scanned back along the eastern bank until they met the red of the rising sun.

Nothing looked familiar. No bluffs, no habitations that he could see, no bridges or roads. It was as if they were alone on a wide sea and would never come to any port. Avoiding the blinding sun, he continued to search the bank for something he could recognize, some sign of life, some signal about where they were going and what lay ahead.

Vaguely it came to him that something did appear familiar, some slight elevation on the horizon, not a hill exactly, but relief, someplace he had seen before, either in life or in a dream. On they floated, and gradually the rise defined itself as a grove of ancient cottonwoods and oaks atop a low rise. He did not want to wake Ruth, because he could not be sure. But on and on they bobbed, and finally, when they were nearly abreast the grove, the chicken house lurched with a jerk and came to rest. The blinding sun was now a great globe of fire, lighting the length of a long, dry sandbar, one he perhaps remembered, reaching out toward them from the land. "Wake up," he shouted to Ruth, shaking her arm. "We've come to rest on the other side."

Then Reuben realized that they were still bound to their sodden vessel by strands of rusting wire. He snapped the wire from its nail and with a single swift motion ripped their bond free and flung it away. Ruth rose up, strong and refreshed from a long sleep, and took Reuben's hand.

Photo by Norma Wilson

Jerry Wilson was born west of the Cimarron River in Oklahoma, near the homesteads two of his great grandfathers claimed in the 1892 Run into Cheyenne Arapaho land. His family worked a marginal sandy farm in a neighborhood of hard-up blacks and whites.

He worked as a farmhand, a handyman, a gas station attendant, an oil field flunkey, a carpenter and a preacher. After two years in the Army and three years teaching in public schools he earned a PhD in English from the University of Oklahoma. There he married poet and fellow student, Norma Clark. They moved to South Dakota, where they "homesteaded" a scrap of the Missouri River bluff, built the geo-solar house where they still live, restored native prairie and raised two kids, Walter and Laura. He taught literature and writing at colleges and universities in Oklahoma and South Dakota before stints as a newspaper journalist, as managing editor of *South Dakota Magazine* and as a county commissioner.

Jerry is the author of three other books: *Blackjacks and Blue Devils*, a collection of Oklahoma stories (Mongrel Empire Press, 2011); *Waiting for Coyote's Call: An Eco-memoir from the Missouri River Bluff* (South Dakota Historical Society Press, 2008); and *American Artery: A Pan American Journey* (Pine Hill Press, 2000). *Across the Cimarron* is his first novel, but one he's been writing in his head since hearing his great grandfather's stories as a child. In semi-retirement he gardens, nurtures prairie, watches his bird and mammal neighbors, and writes when it's too hot or too cold to play outside.

CPSIA information can be obtained
at www.ICGtesting.com
Printed in the USA
FFOW02n0152261117
43677821-42501FF